T0156802

Down in the Dark

MIKE TWEDDLE

iUniverse, Inc.
New York   Bloomington

Down in the Dark

iUniverse books may be ordered through booksellers or by contacting:

iUniverse
1663 Liberty Drive
Bloomington, IN 47403
www.iuniverse.com
1-800-Authors (1-800-288-4677)

Because of the dynamic nature of the Internet, any Web addresses or links contained in this book may have changed since publication and may no longer be valid. The views expressed in this work are solely those of the author and do not necessarily reflect the views of the publisher, and the publisher hereby disclaims any responsibility for them.

ISBN: 978-1-4502-5388-8 (sc)
ISBN: 978-1-4502-5390-1 (ebook)
ISBN: 978-1-4502-5387-1 (dj)

Printed in the United States of America

iUniverse rev. date: 11/19/2010

For Cath, Max and Jake

Mike Tweddle started writing punk and political fanzines, before travelling the world on a shoestring, gaining a 1st class degree in Environmental Technology from Durham University and writing the screenplay for the movie "The Last Blast". Mike lives and works in North East England, where he inspects quarries, mines and waste sites. He lives with Cath and their sons, Max and Jake.

CHAPTER ONE

I'm known as Nelson Rabies round these parts but you'll probably guess that's not my real name. I suppose that should be obvious. I mean it is a pretty stupid name, unless I was the son of some crazy rock star, trust me, that's definitely not the case. Although, according to my Dad, he once played guitar in a punk rock band called Burnin' Bridges. I'm fairly sure that didn't work out, well not unless my Dad was the only successful rock star in history to pack it all up to work on the bins!

No, I actually entered the world fifteen years ago as Nelson Burns, not quite as striking a name, I would agree, but one my folks felt they would be happy with. Where we live in Larkley, a small Dales town in the North of England, believe me being called Nelson is bad enough!

I'll just cut to the chase; the Nelson bit comes from a certain Mr. Mandela, a hero of my Dad's. As for the "rabies" part this recent addition to my title comes courtesy of my best mate Sparky - but more about him later. Anyway, put the two parts together and you have someone who sounds like they should be quarantined on a remote island.

My reason for forced isolation is much simpler – I'm presently excluded from school.

Until very recently I was one of those kids which every school year has, the class clown, the practical joker, the court jester with the big gob, and, as far as most of my teachers are concerned, small brain. But for most of my school career none of that mattered. I mean who cares about getting an A+ for Geography when you can belch in time to the theme from Match of the Day; does it matter if you get a pass for painting a landscape in Art when you can sketch a picture of our art teacher, Miss Swainsby, as you imagine her in the nude (although in my defence it was a very flattering picture), and who gives a flying fajita about Home Economics anyway!

I like to think that I made some good mates at Rockcliffe Comprehensive but I also had my enemies, the bullies and the meatheads. Mind you I was never too worried about gaining the friendship of that particular group whose combined brain cells amounted to less than that of the average garden slug.

However, it was because of one of those very slugs and his relationship to another, apparently more powerful, slug that got me the boot. The slug in question was the school bully, a certain Douglas Spindle, or Doug the Slug to you. The more powerful slug was his father - Harry Spindle, Mayor of Larkley and chair of the governors of Rockcliffe Comprehensive. I guess you can now see how I've got myself into this sticky situation.

Even my faithful hound, the family pet mongrel Kickstart, looks at me these days with a rather resigned expression on his furry mush. I often look at the mangy old fellow and wonder what he is thinking about. I would love to be able to read his thoughts, just what does a dog spend his days thinking about?

He thinks I'm just a daft old mutt who ain't got a thought kicking about in my head. But I'll tell you something, Kickstart might be a flea bitten old bag of fur but everyone seems to want to either feed me or play with me, unlike him. All he seems to do is attract trouble and get shouted at by the bigger humans. Well, I ask you, who is the daft mutt now?

Kickstart started to scratch his midlands and I sat down to think about the mess I now found myself in.

The fateful day came when I was escorted from the school premises with my poor Mum looking like she was walking alongside a war criminal. I couldn't argue with the sentence, a fixed term exclusion of four weeks with the right of appeal. I should have known that to smack Doug the Slug in front of the head-teacher was a mistake, especially since the headmaster happened to be the cousin of Harry Spindle. My hot temper had finally got me into hot water and mainly because I had lost my rag and hit Douglas square on the nose. Mind you, at the time Douglas had been forcing a Year Eight kid to hand over his dinner money.

However, to see Mum trying, and failing, to hold back her tears of shame and disappointment I was suddenly hit by the thought that I had been acting like a complete tool for a long time - and now it was too late.

I could have knuckled down, I could have achieved something but now I was a social leper, shunned by my family, not allowed to mix with other kids because their parents thought I was going to end up as another "good for nothing", and already on the scrap-heap at the grand old age of fifteen.

My Dad could barely look at me when I walked into our sitting room. Instead he looked out of the window for what seemed like an eternity. I was nervous and I could tell my Mum was feeling anxious as she left the room. Even the normally smug face of my older brother Freddy looked uneasy as he suddenly found a copy of "Country Walks" strangely interesting.

"You know your Grandad left school at fifteen," Dad said, still looking out of the window.

I tried to say something but the dryness in my throat felt like I had been gargling sand.

"Yeah, he left school at fifteen." Now Dad turned round and I wished he hadn't. His eyes betrayed his sadness. "Yep, ended up working in the armaments factory for the next twenty five years, while his mates who finished school went on to achieve all sorts and guess what?" I knew the answer to the question and looked down.

"Dead at forty two, his lungs busted by the asbestos in the dust inside the factory they say. But there was one big difference between you and him Nelson – any ideas?"

A tear of self-pity fell from my eye to disappear into the surface of the carpet below.

"He didn't have a choice, he had a family to support. Whereas you've just peed it all away for the sake of a few laughs, using your fists instead of your brain. Nice one son, I'm proud of you."

I wanted my Dad to give me a slap across my stupid head rather than leave the room. It was a good two minutes before Freddy finally chirped up, some kind of record for his foghorn of a mouth.

"Did you know that the Coast to Coast is one of the most popular walks in Western Europe and the Ramblers Association was formed in 1934 and has 139,000 members?"

I looked up to see Freddy raising a knowing eyebrow, in an "I-told-you-so" kind of fashion. Normally I would have reacted but I was painfully aware of where confrontation had got me so far.

"Look, this is serious brown sticky stuff you're up to the neck in but nobody's snuffed it have they?" Freddy declared.

"Not yet I suppose." I agreed reluctantly.

Freddy put the magazine down, stood up and walked towards the door. "There is a way out of this you know."

"Go on then," I said, rolling my eyes skywards as I waited for his suggestion.

"Make them proud of you, it's not too late."

Freddy got up and left the room, leaving me on my own and lost for words.

CHAPTER TWO

The next morning I got out of bed, scratched the bits that needed scratching and looked in the mirror. Maybe this was the first day of the rest of my life, maybe I could make a new start, and maybe I could make something of myself. I had visited the Pupil Referral Unit, or the Unit as I called it, the previous day, where a particularly scary exclusion officer, Miss Steint, had worked out the lesson plan for my exclusion period.

But before that happened a new task lay ahead of me, one that only the bravest soul would dare volunteer for, although the truth was I hadn't actually volunteered!

I strolled down the garden path and looked into the fishpond. I was convinced that a dozen beady eyes looked back at me from within the murky depths. I wasn't even too sure what actually lay in the black water and, although I didn't want to find out, at least Kickstart was doing his bit by drinking it!

Three hours, four goldfish, six frogs and one slightly decomposed Action Man later, the pond was empty. Dad had left me plenty of bin bags, the one and only perk from his job, into which to empty the putrid, black sludge from the bottom of the pond. The fish and frogs were placed into old sweet jars from Dad's shed.

After cleaning the lining with a hosepipe and taking what seemed like an eternity to fill the pond with clean water I gathered the sweet jars, containing various water creatures and the Action Man, into a circle.

"Well troops this is it, this is the time you've been waiting for."

Kickstart looked at me as if I was losing my marbles. But dogs don't think such thoughts – do they?

He seems to be getting crazier by the day. Right now it looks like he's talking to the fish and some kind of tiny pink human? He looks after me well but I do think that he is starting to act like a mad dog. Maybe he's got distemper, or worse, ringworm!

I popped the little creatures back into the lovely, clear water.

"You've lived in dirt and scum for too long, now it's time for you be free, free I say, swim, swim and let the clean ocean currents carry you on to new and wonderful adventures".

Even the mouldy old Action Man was placed back in. I felt he had earned his place in there and besides, his little aquatic mates would probably miss him.

I saluted them before turning to Kickstart.

"Come on, let's get inside and detox your tongue."

As I lifted Kickstart onto the kitchen worktop I turned on the portable TV. I had already checked the clock on the wall and it was within permitted hours. Between midday and one o'clock TV was allowed, when the only real option was the news. I had missed the national stuff but I was soon half listening to the local broadcast as I carefully cleaned poor Kickstart's tongue with an old cloth. The old mutt was nothing if not tough. I still remembered the day when Sparky's little sister, Eloise, who was no more than a year or so old, waddled over to Kickstart, smiled angelically, then bit his nose! Luckily Kickstart's only reaction was a loud yelp of pain. Eloise was too young to describe what a dog's black, spongy muzzle tasted like but, to this day, I still cringe when I think about it!

My attention was grabbed when I heard Harry Spindle's name mentioned by the TV newscaster. His fat, smug face beamed out from the TV screen.

It appeared he was boasting about his waste recycling empire which, so my Dad told me, was a licence to print money. It was workers like my Dad who collected the town's rubbish each day and Harry Spindle, under his Mayor's hat and a hideous gold chain, made a fortune from by recycling. There was something about Spindle's business that my Dad just knew was wrong but he couldn't quite put his finger on it.

Back on the telly the newscaster made Spindle out to be some sort of saviour of the environment. Apparently Larkley Council, despite being bottom of most leagues like education (admittedly I probably hadn't helped with that one), social services and health, was actually one of the leaders in environmental targets. The Council and the waste company who worked for them (and happened to be owned by the Spindle estate) were showing the rest of the UK how to recycle their waste. Something smelt rotten in the kingdom of Spindle – and it wasn't just the rubbish!

A phone began to ring; I knew it wasn't my mobile, since its surrender had been part of the terms of my house arrest. I picked up the house phone.

"Hello?"

"Rabies, greetings it's Sparky, you doing anything?"

"No, just watching the news."

"Good, come over to our house, I've got an idea."

I put the phone back in its cradle and hoped Sparky's idea was going to be one that sat easily within my present restricted lifestyle. Somehow I doubted it would.

CHAPTER THREE

I should explain something about Sammy "Sparky" Hanson; he is my best friend but I know for a fact that he has been changed forever by television, in particular by the type of programmes where contestants somehow become instant business tycoons!

He left school last summer, with the business bug burning inside him and, in his own head, he saw a new image for himself, as king of the hill, with a multi-million pound empire. So far he has accumulated four hundred and twenty eight quid! I was actually impressed by this, considering some of the disasters he has set in motion.

His various business ideas had included central heating for rabbit hutches, coffee-making machines for lorry drivers, and a whistle detection system for finding spectacles. Three singed bunnies, two scalded lorry drivers and sixteen pairs of shattered spectacles later and yet, by some miracle, the jammy dipstick had still managed to save four hundred and twenty eight quid!

The truth of it was that he also had a job down at the local supermarket, shelf stacking. But he assured me that this was just his "stepping stone" into the real world of business!

"Say that again." I asked in total astonishment.

"Yep, you heard me right Nelson."

"Let me get this right, you want me to go with you mining for precious stones." I laughed, hoping to see Sparky do the same!

"You heard right," he said, totally straight faced.

"Come on matey, this ain't South Africa and I don't think there's that many diamond mines around here."

"Who mentioned diamonds?"

Sparky reached into his scruffy little rucksack, and after a long rummage, pulled out an object wrapped in a piece of bright, flowery cloth.

"Isn't that a bit of one of Eloise's dresses?"

I knew I had nearly given the game away. Sparky's little sister Eloise was a fiery thirteen year old with bags of attitude. She was a pain in the backside most of the time but, somehow I enjoyed a good old battle of wits with her. The problem was Sparky knew how I really felt about her which could often make life difficult.

Sparky laughed out loud. "Don't worry, she'd chucked that dress in a charity bag." The smile suddenly dropped from his face. "But don't tell her matey or she'll have my crown jewels for earrings." He was as wary of Eloise's fiery temper as I was.

"So, what exactly you got in there? Emeralds?" I asked.

Sparky carefully unwrapped the object to reveal a small greenish, block.

"This, my friend, is fluorspar." Sparky said enthusiastically.

"Looks more like kryptonite to me."

"Listen Nelson, it could be Superman's snot for all I care; all I know is that, not a million miles away from this very town, in an old abandoned mine, there's a supply of this stuff waiting to be dug up, polished and sold."

"We're not exactly talking rubies here are we?" I said bluntly.

Sparky stood back, his chest puffed out with pride. "No, we're not but, next time your folks let you get anywhere near a computer, check out this stuff. There are plenty of rich Americans, wealthy Arab royal families and affluent Europeans who buy this stuff for stupid money."

We looked at each other before both bursting into laughter.

"It sounds like a right laugh Sparky and I'd love to join you, but there's one major problem – two in fact."

Sparky wrapped the rock back up in the cloth.

"You mean Ma and Pa Rabies? Don't worry I think I've got that covered."

I suddenly had the feeling that my old mate was going to seriously jeopardise any chance of an early escape from my grounding.

CHAPTER FOUR

Harry Spindle came from a long line of businessmen and town councillors in Larkley, who my Dad had often told me would not have looked out of place at a major gangster's trial. I know my Dad was prejudiced, after all Harry was his boss, but I trusted his judgement. He was always the first to admit when he had made a mistake – or dropped a big sweaty one.

I think the main reason for the mutual hatred between Harry and my Dad was due to the fact that Dad was the shop steward for the manual workers at Larkley Council, as well as team leader of his group of Council refuse workers; the same Council that Harold Spindle also happened to be the leader of! Over the years there'd been a couple of incidents thrown into the mix that had definitely nurtured their dislike of one another.

The cause of one strike was a certain Mrs Ethel Grimshaw, one of the local lollipop ladies who had chopped her lollipop pole down from the standard length, breaking the Council's rules and who was then threatened with the sack. In fairness to Mrs Grimshaw she was shorter than most of the Year 1-5 pupils she guided across the road so using the standard lollipop would be like a leprechaun trying to use a lamppost as a walking stick. My Dad got the Council's workers to strike for three days, before the bosses relented and allowed Mrs Grimshaw to use her sawn off pole.

The second case involved one Chester McWinney, a local miner who, after being finished from the pits, had worked as a gardener for the Council. Apparently McWinney was an unusual bloke who liked to fill his house with the rubbish that most people threw away. You've seen the type of place, old fridges in the garden, piles of carrier bags containing everything from old, rusty tools to single shoes, car engines on the porch and the occasional bath tub that has become a haven for local wildlife. When the court order finally came to clean out Chester McWinney's house it was found to contain enough items to keep the whole of e-bay going for a week.

But Mr McWinney's only "crime" was that amongst his bric-a-brac, were four small palm trees planted in four hideous pots that were encrusted with Larkley Council's Coat of Arms. These stunted palm trees had once sat proudly outside the Town Hall or, as my Dad called it, "Spindleland". Mr McWinney had apparently been told that the potted plants were to be thrown in a skip. He had decided that the mini palm trees would be better off in his garden. But upon being found in possession of, what was described in the local paper, the Larkshire Gazette (or "The Spindle Times" as my Dad liked to call it), a "significant amount of stolen Council property" Chester McWinney was brought up on charges of misconduct. My Dad stood up in court and tried to plead his case but, technically, he had been caught with knocked off Council goods and so he was sacked.

My Dad was devastated; he really liked and respected Chester McWinney. He was sure that Harry Spindle's legal cronies had stitched the poor old chap up. My Dad was proved right when, within weeks of Chester McWinney being evicted from his council house, it was quickly snapped up by a "mystery buyer", swiftly done up, and sold for a big, fat profit.

As for Chester McWinney, he just disappeared, like all the stuff from his house. My Dad was convinced the poor old guy had simply slunk away and died of a broken heart. I could tell that it took a long time for my Dad's own heart to mend; such was his guilt for not saving the old chap's job and house.

So now you can see the two opposing teams we have. In the blue corner Mr Harry Spindle, proprietor of an apparently successful waste disposal company, property owner, Town Mayor and complete boghead, and in the red corner, Mr Billy Burns, binman, shop steward and top geezer.

CHAPTER FIVE

"Steady fella," I screamed, as the pickaxe Sparky was presently swinging around his garage came within millimetres of my left ear.

"I reckon this should do the trick; now where was that rope?" Sparky hopped onto an old table and looked in the space above the garage's roof timbers.

"Hurry up Sparky I've gotta get to the pupil referral unit, Miss Steint is expecting me at four."

"What's she like?" Sparky's voice floated down from the space above.

"Ok. Strict I guess but I s'pose she should be."

Sparky's face appeared from above. "No, I mean *what* is she like?"

"Oh I see, well if you like sixty year old ladies, with a wart on her chin, who smells of stale cigs then, yeah, she's okay."

"Who likes sixty year old ladies?"

On hearing Eloise's voice I felt the blood drain from my face and, as I turned around, my worst fears were confirmed.

"Surely not, Nelson, I thought you'd have better taste?" Eloise said, with a worryingly knowing look on her thirteen-year-old face.

"I was talking about my Exclusion Officer- honest!"

I decided to change tactic. "Anyway, how come you're off school? At least, for once, I've got a good excuse."

"Women's problems," Eloise stated.

I wished I hadn't asked.

"You're such a little drama queen Eloise," Sparky declared from above.

"You men have it easy you know." Eloise said defiantly.

"Well now you're here you can help us. You got a torch?" Sparky asked, ignoring his sister's comments.

"What for?" Eloise said.

Sparky jumped down from the table, an old thick rope looped over his shoulder. "If one must know my friend, Mr Nelson Rabies, and I are going to make our fortune in the precious stones industry."

"Yeah, yeah, yeah." Eloise had obviously heard his crazy money making ideas a thousand times.

"Mock if you wish little sister but we intend to set off on such a venture first thing tomorrow."

It appeared that Sparky had clearly transformed into Phileas Fogg.

Eloise looked at both of us momentarily, deciding if we were winding her up or not. "But I thought your big business partner here was under close scrutiny, which kind of kills any chance of travelling to the four corners of the earth to find your fortune."

Sparky put one foot on the table and rested his hand on his hip. He scratched the bumfluff on his chin, as if he was considering whether it was better to trek around, or fly over, the Himalayas!

"That may be true but I have a cunning plan which, if you allow me, I will acquaint you with."

Eloise looked at me and shrugged her shoulders as Sparky continued.

"From tomorrow Nelson Rabies is to start work, albeit part time, for Mr Tommy Ratson, owner of the local scrap and timber emporium."

Sparky had talked to his Uncle who had okayed it for me to work at his yard, which I could squeeze in after my lessons at the pupil referral unit. Of course, I knew this plan was foolhardy but I thought if Mum and Dad were okay with it, they would be, at least, proud of me for trying to work and learn some new skills. As for the mining bit I reckoned it would be best to keep them in the dark for now, at least until we had made our fortune!

Eloise looked at me. "Uncle Tommy? I thought you wanted to be a professional scuba diver, not a gofer in a scrapyard?"

Although she was taking the rise out of me I thought I sensed the slightest hint of disappointment.

"I ain't exactly in a position to choose; besides if my appeal goes belly up I'm gonna need some sort of skills in the big, bad world out there."

"The skill of keeping out of trouble would be a good start." Eloise said, without the remotest hint of sarcasm.

"It's time the lad found out about the real world and, besides Uncle Tommy's yard is going to be very handy indeed." Sparky proclaimed, like the world conqueror he thought he was.

"So will these do?" Eloise said, holding up two small lights attached to headbands, that she used for rollerblading around the streets of Larkley.

"Perfect," said Sparky, but before he could take hold of them his sister held them back.

"You can have them if you tell me where and when you're going?"

Sparky shook his head and snatched the torches from Eloise's hand. "No way, it's too dangerous." He put the torches in his pocket.

As we left the garage I turned briefly to see the look of disappointment on Eloise's face and I felt pretty rotten.

CHAPTER SIX

I had to get to the Unit sharpish; I didn't want to rock a boat, that was already heading for the rocks.

I had successfully completed my first mission by collecting all my text books from home, although I'm sure the SAS never had this problem; a potentially seething Mum waiting for them, ready to dish the punishment should they return from some war-torn country, having eliminated a dictator or something. Then again, they probably hadn't been stupid enough to get thrown out of school!

I was peddling pretty fast down the high street, having turned at the swimming baths and headed down the steep bank towards the Unit. The weight of several text books in my rucksack made the descent considerably quicker. I was crouched over the handlebars of my bike, keeping it as stable as possible in the high-speed descent. I could see the industrial estate at the bottom of the bank, with the tall towers of SWG (Spindle's Waste Group) dominating the skyline. The referral unit was further down the bank. All I had to do was maintain my trajectory and speed and I would make it in time.

As I neared the main junction I looked right and left to see that the coast was clear- and went for it.

It was probably about the middle of the junction when I noticed the enormous metal grill of the black 4 x 4. Unfortunately the grill was, at that point, about two feet away from my back wheel!

Somehow, although my bike decided to fly in one direction and me in the other, I escaped with a busted mudguard and a grazed knee.

As I picked the bike up I sensed that someone was approaching me quickly. I looked up to see the red, startled face of the Mayor of Larkley – Harry Spindle.

"You okay son?"

I checked myself. "Yep, but maybe you should stick to the speed limit Mayor Spindle."

Spindle's face turned purple. "What? Me? You cheeky little beggar. It was you who shot across that junction."

"I've done it a million times and I've never been siderocketed before." I declared proudly.

Harry Spindle's chubby cheeks looked like they were about to explode. "I've got a good mind to call the police?"

"Oh yes, maybe we should." I said defiantly, although I had no real intention of calling his bluff. I knew it was my fault and I was in enough trouble with, what seemed like, the whole world.

"But I never saw you, you came out of nowhere." Spindle barked.

I seized the advantage. "So you weren't looking then?" Over the years my Dad had told me that people usually trip themselves up with their own, often daft, words.

"I didn't say that," he said, with an obvious tremble in his voice and it was only then I detected the slight unpleasant smell of beer on his already gruesome breath.

The passenger door of the black 4 x 4 opened and a muscular man, wearing sunglasses, poked his huge, shaven head out. From where I was standing it appeared that this bloke's neck was as thick as his head.

"Harry, get in zee car now," the neckless wonder said in a strange accent.

"You're lucky to be alive young fella, be more careful in future can you!" Harry quickly returned to the car and got in.

As they drove away the driver stared long and hard at me. I gave him my stupidest smile, which I knew would annoy him. The guy took his sunglasses off to reveal the coldest eyes I had ever seen.

I shuddered and turned away before getting back on my slightly buckled bike to make the journey to the referral unit.

CHAPTER SEVEN

I peddled to the referral unit as fast as my buckled front wheel would allow. I dumped my bike on the path and ran towards the unit's front entrance, looking at my watch. It was tight. Mum appeared at the door holding her arm up so I could see the face of her watch.

"Just, buster, just. Now hurry up Miss Steint is waiting"

Mum signed me in and I followed her into a small classroom where Miss Steint was sitting behind a desk, drinking a cup of tea. I noticed the teacup seemed quite small in her huge, strong hands.

"You get those books Nelson?" my Mum asked.

"Yeah, I've got them all."

"That's a good start on the long road to redemption young man." Miss Steint's voice boomed so loudly I was sure I could see mini-tidal waves appearing in the aquarium behind her.

"Sit down Nelson we need to discuss your future." I wouldn't have been surprised if right then and there she'd donned a small, black cap and condemned me to the gallows.

I looked at my Mum who was wearing the same doom–laden expression.

"Are you aware of the seriousness of your situation?" Miss Steint asked.

I resisted the temptation to come up with a sarcastic comment.

"Yes, I do and I want to put it right."

"You should have thought about that while you were acting the goat for the past two years," Mum said.

"Indeed that is the case Mrs Burns. But we find ourselves now in this position and we can't go back in time so I have set out a plan for you Nelson."

"I hope it's a cunning one." I said.

The way Miss Steint arched her left eyebrow was the equivalent of saying, "Don't you dare mess with me little man, or I will crush you, crush you like the tiny beetle you are."

"And there is still my appeal?" I offered.

"Yes there is still hope, he may be a numpty but we can't write him off just yet," said Mum,

Miss Steint looked at me without any sign of emotion. "The way you're heading young man you'll be lucky if you end up working down the abattoir."

"But I'm a vegetarian." I stuttered.

"I'm afraid your dietary needs, or sensitivities regarding animals are no longer relevant and I'm sure your Mother will agree with me."

"I'm a vegetarian as well Miss Steint and no son of mine is going to work in an abattoir," Mum declared firmly.

Mum looked at me and I could see the slightest twinkle in her eye. "Well let's concentrate on your education for now Nelson," Miss Steint said, rising to her feet. Even though I was reasonably tall for my age she towered above me like some kind of colossal troglodyte.

"Thank you for your time Mrs Burns, I will be contacting you to arrange the twenty hours per week of education that Nelson is required, by law, to receive."

She turned sharply on her heels and walked to the front door. "We are all relying on you to do the right thing Nelson."

As we stepped through the doors into the sunshine outside I turned to face Mum. We held each other's gaze for a few moments before bursting into laughter.

Eventually Mum controlled herself. "This doesn't get you off the hook mister, you're still grounded and still on probation."

"I know Mum, and besides I have Sergeant Major Steint to take care of me."

Once again we burst out laughing.

"Shut up you dingbat and go and see your Dad. He's down at his allotment and wants some help."

I resisted the temptation to salute her, I didn't want to chance my luck and it had been the first time we had laughed together in ages, something we used to do a lot before I got into trouble.

CHAPTER EIGHT

The way to the allotments could be easy or difficult, depending on how adventurous I was feeling. There was the straightforward way, which took me around the town and eventually onto the bridge across the river, but that road arched round for about two long, boring miles. The other way was straight down to the river, through the woods, and involved fighting my way through a plantation of treacherous hawthorn bushes, hitching my bike over my shoulder and attempting to cross a large and rather slimy green metal pipe that spanned the river about ten foot below.

Dad had first shown me the short cut when I was about seven. The only hazards back then had been natural ones. In the years since newer more sinister dangers had developed: one in particular that went by the name of Chucker Wilson.

Colin "Chucker" Wilson was a kid who had been permanently excluded from Rockcliffe Comprehensive a couple of years ago. He had been named "Chucker" not for his ability to throw a cricket ball, or javelin but because the huge, brutish lump was renowned for throwing any fellow pupils who annoyed him in any direction he felt fit to do so.

Since his exclusion Chucker had rarely been seen in the town where he used to roam. Instead, sightings of him generated from the surrounding woods and hills like some kind of deranged teenage Big Foot. As far as I knew he had been booted out by his folks and was living rough in the woods, through which I was about to ride my bike.

I looked down the steep track that led into the woods and felt the tightness in my stomach rising rapidly. I set off and, before I knew it, I was half way down the track and heading for the tricky slalom, through a thick covering of razor sharp hawthorns.

I stopped at a felled tree which lay across the path when, out of the blue, I thought I heard a noise in the nearby undergrowth. Up to now I had been travelling fast, which had held my fear back but now all sorts of chilling thoughts began to barge their way into my mind, as I realised I was in the heart of the blackness of the forest. Was that a tree I saw to my left, or the bloodied figure of Chucker Wilson, waiting to devour me as the main course? I looked again and realised, with relief, that it was just a tree so I decided to push on in through the hawthorns.

I could hear the river somewhere in front of me and pressed on, hoping that I could smash my way through the thicket to relative safety on the other side. Suddenly I could see strands of daylight through the bushes and this spurred me on. With one last gallant effort I pressed forward. I realised I was going too fast and tried to hit the brakes only to impale myself on a wall of spikes.

I edged my way slowly out of the thick hawthorn bush and was nearly free when I heard the crack of a twig behind me. Was somebody there? I waited for several heart-bursting moments and the silence was unbearable. Was my attacker waiting for the right moment or had I just imagined it? The next crack from the darkness was enough to push me into, literally, ripping myself out of the bush, getting on my bike, freewheeling down to the pipe, that spanned the river, and crossing it still holding my bike. Without putting a foot wrong I jumped onto the other bank and peddled away furiously. I didn't bother looking back.

I also didn't notice the three other bikes on the path in front of me until I smashed into them.

Douglas Spindle was not a happy bunny today; then again he was always a miserable sap.

"Look what you've done to my bike Burns, Dad just bought me this model from the States."

I looked at the gaudy, brightly coloured monstrosity that Douglas was moping over.

"Classy Douglas, very classy." I said mockingly. Both Douglas and the two cronies hanging out with him seemed to think I really was complimenting his tasteless mount. Surely it was obvious I was taking the rise!

Douglas stepped off his bike and handed it to one of his cronies. It would appear that, just like his Dad, he had a small army of people who thought the sun shone out of his rear end.

"Well, you wouldn't know class if it fell on you from outer space Burns."

"Speaking of which have you visited your home planet recently Douglas?"

The smile dropped from his chubby face and he stepped right up to me. He was obviously feeling a bit cockier with his chums beside him.

"How's life these days Nelson? I know I prefer school without you hanging around."

"I miss the old place, the banter, my friends, even some of the classes but you know what I miss most?"

"What would that be?" Douglas asked smugly.

"Seeing a bullyboy like you, who won't pick on anyone above the age of twelve in case you get turned over by them!"

"Well, how about you and me, right here, right now Burns?"

"You had a bravery pill Dougie?"

I could see Douglas shaking with anger. He was trying to goad me into starting a fight, no doubt to get me into further trouble.

"Soz Doug I refuse to have a battle of the wits with someone who's unarmed."

Douglas frowned in confusion, before smiling slyly.

"Well, I guess morale in your house must be pretty low, you being chucked outta school and your Dad working the bins for my Dad!"

This was the moment, if there was to be a moment, when I could react. I closed my eyes and imagined I had a kung fu master watching over me, who although shaven headed and dressed in brightly coloured robes, looked a lot like Sparky!

"Bend with the wind not break like the willow," Zen Master Sparky said, in a rather poor Chinese accent that had more than a tinge of Northern English.

"Thanks Douglas."

"For what?" He asked in confusion.

"Talking to a slug like you always makes me feel a lot better about myself."

Douglas made a portly lunge for me but I was already peddling away.

"I'm gonna get you Nelson Burns, get you good you hear me."

Yeah, yeah I thought, ignoring the threat I had heard on a daily basis for the past five years or so.

CHAPTER NINE

"What in the name of Mother Nature has happened to you lad?" my Dad asked, as I pulled up at the old, rusty gates of his allotment.

I looked at my reflection in one of the glass panes in his greenhouse. I was covered in bits of hawthorn, scratched all over, my hair looked like it had been plugged into the mains and my bike had not fared much better.

"Just the perils of riding a pushbike in today's modern, hasty society."

"Well, I would suggest being a comedian won't exactly enhance your chances of survival."

I was obviously still in the eye of the storm with both my Mum and Dad.

"I got caught up in the bushes over the other side of the river."

"You been to see Miss Steint?" Dad asked suspiciously.

"Yeah, she's sorting out my lessons and reckoned I would end up working in the abattoir!"

"Ha, I can imagine your mother's reaction to that!" My Dad wasn't a vegetarian but he knew, and respected, how strongly my Mum felt about her beliefs. "There wasn't any blood spilt was there?"

"Not yet!"

It was then I noticed a huge pile of grass and vegetable cuttings that were piled up in Dad's allotment. It seemed Dad had managed to cram several tonnes of green waste into the tiny space. His rows of cabbages, leeks and onions were, of course, left untouched but any other available space had been taken over.

Dad noticed me scanning the mountainous green heap.

"I've started a new venture Nelson. What you see before you is the beginning of a new dawn for Larkley. I'm starting a composting scheme amongst all the keen gardeners and allotment owners in Larkley. But it will be a collective, with any profits shared equally."

I looked around at the massive, steaming heap. "Looks more like a mountain of green rubbish to me Dad."

"There be gold in dem dare hills me lad," Dad said, squinting one eye and sounding slightly bonkers.

"Really? And maybe we can swap some of your chicken plop for gold bars!"

"You don't believe me do you?" Dad's voice sounded more serious now. "How do you think the likes of Harry Spindle and his cronies have made all their millions?"

"I thought his real money had been made buying and selling houses?"

My Dad rolled his eyes. "Yeah, in the beginning but he soon realised that since the environment has now become the burning issue, excuse the pun, of the day, he knew that real, big money could be had."

"And he started like this?" I said, hoping I didn't sound too dismissive.

"No, he never had any intention of starting like this. Harry Spindle has two huge aerobic digester towers which turn out nothing as good, or organic, as proper compost." I could tell my Dad was starting to get angry just mentioning Harry's name.

I didn't really understand the technical stuff regarding the huge towers in Harry Spindle's factory but I knew that he had the contract to collect all the household rubbish from the town. Council's were no longer allowed to landfill any waste. Instead companies like the Spindle Waste Group were contracted to recycle huge amounts of green waste. At his factory Spindle had recently had two huge towers constructed. Apparently they worked like big ovens. Green waste was put through the towers, which heated the material up, and produced a product at the end of the process which was known as GIP (Garden Improvement Product). My Dad called this material "fluff" because no gardener in their right mind would use it as compost on their own land.

Harry Spindle was reaching the highest recycling targets in the North of England. He was able to take the vast amount of waste his company collected from bin wagons, operated by blokes like my Dad, to his factory and at the end of it, show fantastic recycling figures. It was like eating as many cakes, pies and chips as you can for a week and having the smallest poo in the world after the seventh day.

"So what you going to do with all this?" I said, looking at Dad's green mountain of waste.

"Step this way son." Dad said, as he walked through the gates across the overgrown path and stopped in front of another set of rusty gates. He placed a key in the ancient padlock and, after a few moments of jiggling the key, it popped open. He pushed the gate open and I followed him through.

On the other side of the gate was a large area of dense, unkempt land with a couple of corrugated buildings that were listing at impossible angles. No one had stepped into this place for a long, long time.

"What do you think?" Dad said proudly.

"Well I reckon if you look hard enough you'll probably find an undiscovered tribe that has been living here happily for the past thousand years without being disturbed."

"No clever dick, I mean what do you think of this as the site where we are going to start our own composting company and take Harry Spindle head on."

I smiled. "Well I guess even the smallest company has to start somewhere, although maybe in more attractive places."

"Listen, the allotment club actually owns this land Nelson. All we have to do is to make sure there is a drainage system in, a collection tank for any fluids, and we don't cause any odour problems to the nearby residents."

I peered over the hedge. "There aren't any nearby residents?"

"Exactly. We've got Big Lol's son, who is some planning expert to put our application together, pay the fee to the Council and wait for them to give us the go ahead."

And that was when I saw the big gaping hole in my Dad's dream. "Harry Spindle's the head of the Council; he isn't gonna give you the go ahead to compete against his own company."

"True Nelson but Big Lol's son has looked at our application and he says that the Council will struggle to find grounds to refuse it, and legally, if they do, we have the right to appeal and get all costs awarded against them when we win."

My Dad was far too excited and I didn't want to spoil his moment. "Good luck Dad."

"Thanks son, anyway I hear you can start part time down at Tommy Ratson's yard?"

"What do you think about it?"

Dad thought for a moment. "Well he may be crazier than a chipmunk on energy drink but he runs a good business up there."

I was pleased Dad approved, but I wondered if Tommy Ratson really was as mad as everyone kept telling me. I guess I would soon find out for myself!

CHAPTER TEN

The class work at the referral unit was very similar to actually being at school itself. The only difference was the mixture of "one to one" lessons and more normal lessons alongside other excluded kids who seemed to suffer from everything from dyslexia to ADHD. I knew that most people probably thought I was as much a boghead as the rest of my new classmates; they were probably right. I just got my head down, something I should have done at real school, and got on with the work that I had been set.

The most interesting lesson was the art class. My update of the Mona Lisa was, at least in my opinion, a classic. I thought she looked good as a psychotic clown!

After a few mind-numbing hours of computer studies and maths I was allowed to escape. I collected Kickstart and we set off to Tommy Ratson's yard.

The yard was everything and more than I had expected. It was a combination of old, crumbling buildings, pallets of sawn timber stacked at impossible heights and old, rotting carcasses of long forgotten family cars. There was also the strangest looking yard dog I had ever seen.

When I saw "Zombie" for the first time I realised that Kickstart was the Brad Pitt of the dog world. Zombie was half dog, half bear, with a sprinkling of werewolf probably chucked in for good measure. He was enormous and made Kickstart, who was not exactly the smallest dog in the world, seem like a small hamster by comparison. He must have weighed 150 pounds and was about a metre wide. But they were not his least redeeming features, for Zombie was a one eyed, three legged, drooling, listing-to-the-right-at-an-unfeasible-angle, huge jawed dog.

Kickstart and I pushed ourselves against a wall as Zombie noticed us and moved with incredible speed, for a tripod dog, to stand directly in front of us.

It was only then I noticed that Zombie was actually wagging what remained of his tail. Kickstart had obviously noticed this before I did and was doing that sniffing thing that dogs do to each other's parts. Once again I wondered what they might be saying to one another.

"So it's you, the one and only Zombie. I've heard so many stories about you Dog."

"Aye, young one, it is I, dog of legend and owned by no man, and what's your name?"

"Kickstart, don't ask why 'cos I don't know. So are all these tales true then?"

"Well they call me Zombie 'cos I came a long time ago from the island of Haiti, where black magic and zombies are the stuff of legend."

"How come you ended up here in this big dirty yard?"

"I was a pirate's dog for a long time, too long, hence the reason a few bits of ol' Zombie be missing. I sailed the seven seas, got involved in raids and fights in which I was lucky to survive never mind lose a few body parts."

"All the dogs round these parts think you're a psycho, a hell hound who will bite you in half if you so much as sniff in their direction."

"Ol' Zombie's as friendly as a puppy but as tough as a wolf when I need to be and by heck I've had to be."

"What you mean?"

"Gypsy camps, fairgrounds, biker yards, scrapyards, fights with hammerhead sharks, wolves and wild boars, it's been a tough old journey but it's been the greatest dog adventure and I wouldn't swap it, or want any of my missing parts back, for any of it."

"Maybe you can tell me about it all."

"One day Kickstart, one day."

Kickstart and Zombie were yapping and yelping at one another, as if they really were having a conversation. But that would be crazy, wouldn't it?

I slowly offered my upturned palm to Zombie who looked at me with his one black eye before licking my hand with what I was sure was not a tongue, but the roughest bit of sandpaper you could buy. I started to laugh as I remembered that old saying about dogs resembling their owners. There was no way that any human being on this planet could look like......

"You must be Billy's lad?"

Yep, sure enough there was the largest man I had ever clapped eyes on. Okay he had all his limbs, but he was missing half an ear and had a huge scar running from his forehead to his chin!

"Don't worry 'bout ol' Zombie. He's a big softy during work hours. You just don't wanna meet him when we close shop."

I finally released my grip on the wall. "Hello Mr Ratson I'm Nelson."

"First rule; it's Tommy okay, second rule is get your work done and you can go home, third is don't get squashed if you can help it. I ain't got time to clean your guts up. Agreed?"

"Agreed" I went to shake his hand. I say hand, but it was more like a shovel, and it was missing a thumb and at least one and a half fingers.

Tommy had obviously noticed as I stared at his rather mangled hand. "That's what happens when you don't watch what you're doing lad."

"Did you lose them in a saw or something?"

"Na lost them in a card game, talk about throwing your hand in eh!" Tommy's laugh sounded like a passing freight train.

"So why did you get chucked out of the boot camp?"

"Boot camp," I asked in confusion.

"School, boot camp, prison they're all the same – trust me I should know."

I gulped. "I was a clown for too long and it ended in disaster."

Tommy checked me out with his dark eyes, as did Zombie with his one deep, black one. "Well, I believe everyone deserves a second chance, I got one, so even a dingbat like you should have one."

He pulled a rolled up cigarette out of his oily jacket.

"Listen, your tasks are simple, clear out that old shed over there and stack the wood you can lift onto those pallets. If ya stack ten pallets ya can jump ship for the day."

"Thanks Mr Rat...., sorry Tommy."

"And then maybe you can join young Sparky and become mining millionaires eh?"

I should have known that Sparky had told his Uncle the score; they were a happy, but rather crazy family.

CHAPTER ELEVEN

By three thirty I had loaded nearly six pallets but I was completely shattered. I steadied myself against the wall and gulped down a full bottle of water in one go. I lay on top of a stack of timber, feeling like my lungs were on fire and my arms and legs were made of cast iron. Chemistry, religious education and even maths seemed a better choice at that stage. Even Kickstart regarded me with a sympathetic expression on his face.

Tommy appeared at the other end of the yard and seemed to be making his way toward me; it appeared that he was using a space hopper for a game of football with Zombie. It was a strange sight indeed.

The fact that the space hopper had one of its horns missing made me think that maybe they too looked like their owners.

"You okay hotshot?" The booming voice of Tommy Ratson made me jump straight to my feet, despite the pain in my legs.

"Yeah, just having a breather Tommy, sorry."

"Don't be sorry you've worked ya nads off. You've done the work of a fully grown man," he looked at the pallets, "in fact you've done more work than some of the old skivers I normally employ. Well done."

Tommy slapped me across the back sending me stumbling over Zombie.

He picked me up effortlessly with his thumbless hand.

"Maybe tomorrow'll be easier."

I looked at him in utter disbelief. "How'd you figure that out?"

"Well if you can manage all this by hand imagine what it would be like if I gave you a pallet trolley to move them."

I was momentarily speechless. "Trolley? Why didn't you mention that first thing this morning?"

"Consider it a test."

"A test to break my back maybe."

"Ha, I like you young fella, you've got attitude." He looked at me knowingly. "Which is probably why you're here in the first place, eh, ha."

Tommy picked up the space hopper and gave it an almighty boot into the yard. I watched it sailing down like an escape pod from a toy space station in the sky. "See you tomorrow young Mr Burns." Tommy walked off into the yard, with Zombie lurching ahead at a top-heavy angle hunting for the space hopper.

"Come on Kickstart, time for the next instalment of my insanity." I said, trundling out of the yard.

As I looked back I noticed Tommy had accidentally dropped a small bottle of golden-coloured liquid from his pocket. He casually picked the bottle up before continuing and singing *"I fought the law, and the law won,"*

My Mum was spot on as usual; he really was a nice bloke who was just a little bit bonkers.

CHAPTER TWELVE

Riding my bike up the relatively long hill, towards the old mine, made me feel like I was on the Tour de France and I had been cycling for two weeks solid. My legs were like concrete. I lifted my bike over the locked gate and pushed it up the hill.

The mine entrance was at the top of an impossibly steep road. Apparently the pot-holed track had once served as the access road for trucks that used to trundle down, laden with the limestone and fluorspar that had been ripped out of the hilltop. There must have been a few white knuckle rides when some of those old trucks, loaded with several tonnes of rock, had trouble stopping at the bottom of that hill as the brakes proved to be less than up to the job.

At the top of the hill were two heavily overgrown tracks. One was much wider and Sparky told me it led to the old limestone quarry on the other side of the hill. The second track was much smaller and a rusty, padlocked gate was the only sign that there had ever been any human activity. A few hundred metres along the path and suddenly the trees cleared to reveal a scene that wouldn't have looked out of place in an episode of Scooby Doo! There were a couple of corrugated iron sheds that had probably once served as the office and canteen for the workers. Beyond them were three sets of the ricketiest, most rotten wooden steps that snaked their way up to the mine entrance which was set back into the quarry face. The skinny mine entrance was almost hidden by thick undergrowth and had "keep out" and "danger" signs nailed across the opening. The only sign of life were the rabbits that darted from hole to hole whenever I took a step and whom Kickstart insisted on chasing.

I climbed the three sets of steps, the occasional creak making each step a potential heart stopper and eventually reached the flat area in front of the mine entrance. There were two rusted rails leading into the dark mouth of the mine. Outside the entrance an old, rusted cart was standing at the end of the rail, most certainly never to move again.

I noticed that, apart from a couple of rickety, old wooden boards, the mine entrance was open and as I looked into the darkness I suddenly realised just how secluded and isolated this place was.

I peered into the darkness of the opening, transfixed by the blackness and was sure, just for a moment, I saw something move. I tried not to panic, after all it was probably just a rabbit but as I looked again I realised whatever was moving back there was much bigger than any rabbit I had ever seen.

"Nelson Rabies is that youuuuuuuu?" the voice rumbled on in a deep, non-human kind of way. I stumbled over and as I looked up I saw what appeared to be the ghost of an old miner. He was standing at the edge of the mine entrance. He was wearing an old miner's hat and boiler suit and was covered in grey dust. The light on his helmet was still turned on; a strap on bicycle light- just like Eloise had given her brother – Sparky.

"You nearly papped your pants there matey." Sparky roared, as he let out a laugh that echoed along the valley.

"Come on in Rabies, I got something to show you," he said.

"Don't do that again you stupid boghead."

"And you wouldn't have done the same?"

He had a point but I wanted to play the wounded solider - at least for a moment.

"Bad day at the office Mister Rabies?"

"You could say that. Don't expect too much from me tonight matey."

Sparky patted me on the shoulder. "Did he pull the old you can use the trolley tomorrow trick?"

I looked at Sparky in amazement, realising that he was as crafty as his Uncle Tommy.

"Guess that's the test he uses all the time?"

Sparky nodded. "Sometimes, although I've seen him just set Zombie on those he has found skiving before."

"That sure is one hell of a dog. What does he feed it on?"

"Kids excluded from school normally."

I threw a small rock at Sparky but it missed him and rolled into the entrance of the mine.

"So you got much done?"

"Nah, I've only been here half an hour; the world of shelf stacking was extra hectic today and they needed me to finish the pet food display for a special offer on cat munchies."

"The pressure of high-end business eh?"

"Yeah, something like that." Sparky looked a little defeated. "Nevermind we can make a proper start tomorrow. By then you should have arms and legs strong enough to cart a few pounds of fluorspar around."

Suddenly he sprang to his feet. "Anyway I've got some cracking tools, check these babies out."

He opened a tool belt to reveal hammers and chisels of all shapes and sizes.

"Where the hell did you get these from? Didn't steal them from the Larkley Mining Centre did you?"

Sparky looked insulted. "An on-line auction of course! I've got some hard hats, Eloise's head torches, rope, all sorts of tools so that we can make a fortune in this little goldmine, sorry fluorspar, mine?"

A thought suddenly bulldozed into my frazzled brain. "Just a question, Bill Gates. Do you know who this "goldmine" actually belongs to because they might have something to say about us chipping away without actually asking their permission?"

"Oh didn't I tell you?" Sparky said, with false innocence.

"Who is it Sparky?" I snapped, but I had the horrible feeling that I already knew.

"Harry Spindle." Sparky said quietly.

"Oh great, I mean thank god it could've been worse - not."

"He never comes up to this place; he's too busy with his waste empire to worry about a few bits of shiny rock. So we may as well take advantage."

"Okay, but if I see that chubby, red face of his anywhere near this place we make an exit sharpish."

"Of course," Sparky agreed, although I doubted he would be that co-operative.

CHAPTER THIRTEEN

Later that afternoon I rolled up at my Dad's allotment but there was very little activity, in fact it felt spookily quiet.

Normally the "gardens" were a hive of activity, with blokes of all ages digging, cutting, hammering and hoeing to make sure their little kingdoms were going to produce the best vegetables in town.

But there was no-one around apart from Old Jed who, the same as every day of the year, no matter the weather conditions, was sat upon the rickety steps of his empty pigeon loft. He was rolling a scraggy cigarette and staring out onto the overgrown vegetable patches within his allotment that had not grown anything edible for many a year. My Dad told me that Old Jed was never really bothered about flying pigeons, or growing food, he sat on those steps every day in order to escape his nagging wife, who apparently was a real dragon in an apron. My Dad told me that there were several blokes who went down the allotments to wile away the hours because it was peaceful and they could be the masters of their own little kingdoms.

"Ey up Nelson." Old Jed rasped, in a voice as decayed as his pigeon loft.

"Hello Jed, bit quiet today. Where's everyone?"

Old Jed studied me with a puzzled look on his craggy face. "You haven't heard son?" He said in the way that people do when they know that they know something you don't know.

"Heard what?" I said, knowing I was about to find out what he knew.

Old Jed finished rolling his cigarette, seeming to take an eternity. "Your old man was taken away by the Bobbies this morning, something about stealing."

I felt the panic rising in my stomach. "Cops? Stealing? My Dad? No way, they've made some kind of mistake.

Old Jed lit his fragile fag, half of which seemed to disappear in the flames. "No doubt about that son."

I jumped on my bike, and started to pedal. The pain I'd felt from toiling down at the yard now forgotten and replaced by the energy of the panic I felt throughout my body.

CHAPTER FOURTEEN

The crowd was made up of about six of Dad's mates from the allotments. It didn't look like a full-scale riot was imminent just yet.

"Free the Larkley One," Big Lol, a fellow bin man and gardener, shouted at the top of his thunderous voice.

Since Dad was nowhere to be seen I quickly realised just who the "Larkley One" was.

"The devils have got him inside Nelson. We're showing him our support." Big Lol said, as I joined the crowd.

Big Lol stepped forward. "Gardeners of the world unite," he bellowed.

I looked around and noticed a reporter from the Larkley Gazette. He was making notes in a small notebook, albeit rather indifferently. Obviously he wasn't expecting too much of a scoop today.

"Looks like Sky News have got their work cut out eh!"

I turned around to see Eloise surveying the scene.

"I heard about your Dad. Apparently he's been arrested for stealing Council property." Eloise said sympathetically.

I looked towards the police station. "What's he supposed to have nicked?"

"Green waste." Lol said, anger apparent in his voice.

"What - compost?" I asked in amazement.

Lol nodded his head. "Grass clippings and hedge trimmings. The Council are saying he has stolen stuff that should have gone into their recycling bins"

"He told me all the compost stuff he got was donated from the lads, their families and friends." I pleaded.

Lol leaned over us. "It was poor Billy who set up the idea of a composting company down at the allotments."

"And the only person round here who thinks such a little company could possibly threaten him is………"

Eloise's eyes lit up. "Mayor Harry Spindle!"

The three of us looked at one another in knowing silence; a combination of gentle nods, raised eyebrows and upturned mouths telling the story.

"Why should Spindle see my Dad and his mates as some kind of threat?"

It didn't add up; there was something very fishy about this but before I had chance to talk about it Big Lol suddenly lurched forward, his huge bulk sending all three of us crashing in the same direction.

"Billy, Billy don't worry lad we're gonna break you out son. These dogs can't keep you in."

I saw my Dad walking out of the police station and through the small crowd, towards us. He looked embarrassed and uncomfortable. He was a private man and this would have been his worst nightmare.

"Thanks for the support lads, I've been charged with stealing council property and have to appear before the magistrates next week."

Lol erupted furiously. "Never. This is an injustice. Let's smash the doors down. Let's turn the cars over, lets….."

My Dad stretched upwards to put a hand on his friend's massive shoulder. "That's no answer is it Lol? Let's all go home. I've got legal aid, so when we get to court it'll all come out in the wash."

"Well, me and the lads are going on strike from tomorrow. So let's see who picks up the green waste then eh."

"Thanks, lads but you really don't have to do that," my Dad said proudly.

"We should Billy," Lol replied, "mates stick together, but you're the man and it's your call."

My Dad turned to me. "You shouldn't be here son."

"I wanted to see you." I said quietly.

"And I'm grateful for that Nelson, but the last place you should be is here, in this atmosphere. Besides, your Mum will be expecting you."

I could sense the warmth in his steady, strong voice. "So pop on your bike and tootle off, but take young Eloise home first."

Once again I felt quite useless but what could I do? As I started to walk off, alongside Eloise, I looked back to see Dad smiling, as best a smile as he could muster in the circumstances.

CHAPTER FIFTEEN

I pushed my bike along the road trying to come up with something, anything, to say.

As we walked past the bright orange gates of the Spindle Waste Group's recycling centre Eloise suddenly spoke up.

"I still don't really know what they do in there."

I thought about using the "eating for seven days and having the smallest poo" theory but decided against it. "I know that he takes a load of waste from the town's dustbins, puts them through some sort of big oven, bakes it and creates a kind of compost that is a tenth of the volume it was." I explained.

"Kind of like eating non stop for a week and only having a tiny poo at the end of it."

I stopped and looked at Eloise.

"What?" she asked bewilderedly.

"Nothing, it's just sometimes you can be really spooky."

"Oh thanks pal," she said, stopping to face me," and what about other times then?"

"Er, what do you mean?"

"What do you think of me the rest of the time?"

Please, let the earth open up and allow me to fall into the fiery depths below. "Er, I think you're okay."

Eloise raised an eyebrow. "Okay, well I guess I should take that as a compliment."

"Listen Eloise, I don't know where this is going but I'm probably not the best person to hang around with at the moment."

"What? You think you're public enemy number one now do you? You haven't exactly committed mass murder, so keep a lid on it."

We carried on walking and the silence descended again, although this time Eloise's infectious giggling quickly broke it. "Spooky, me? You really are a wuss Nelson Rabies you know that."

I also started to laugh.

Eloise smiled. "You may be a complete saddo, but you ain't exactly an inmate on death row –yet!"

"Thanks, I'm trying to get myself back on the right track and make my folks proud of me for the first time in a long while."

"So this little mining expedition with my fool of an older brother, is that gonna make your folks proud, or get you in more bother?"

She had a point, but a bit of harmless fun was irresistible, especially if I could keep my nose clean, do the class work at the Unit and do my duties at the yard. "Na, it's gonna be our future, especially now that I ain't gonna be a brain surgeon!"

She chuckled, a rather nice chuckle. "My brother is crazy, but he is stubborn and hard working, so it may just work out, you never know."

She looked away. "Either that or you two really will be spending your next holiday on death row."

CHAPTER SIXTEEN

By the time I got home my Dad was already there.

I expected to get a right rollocking, but my Mum just told me to take Kickstart outside for his weekly scrub. It was obvious that they were intending to "have a talk" as adults do, which meant that the presence of any kids was not welcome.

Now giving Kickstart a clean is like trying to give a contender from Extreme Fighting a makeover: not easy! He could normally sense when the hosepipe and dog shampoo were coming out.

I found him under the conifers and gently dragged him onto the cracked concrete area underneath the outside tap.

"I'm only trying to clean you up, you smelly old git."

I can never understand why he insists on rubbing this frothy stuff in my fur which smells like a flowerbed! I like my own smell, that smell that tells other dogs who I am. These humans prefer to smell like anything rather than themselves, as if they are ashamed of their own odours – how strange!

As I rubbed the shampoo into Kickstart's back I could hear the raised voices of my folks coming through the open window of the sitting room.

"What were you thinking Billy?" my Mum yelled

I could sense my Dad's discomfort from where I was kneeling. "I haven't done anything wrong. Don't you believe me Louise?"

"Oh course I believe you; you didn't steal anything, I just can't believe you were so naïve."

I looked at Kickstart who looked back in similar discomfort. Did he understand, or did he have shampoo in his eyes?

"That compost doesn't belong to the bleeding Council. I've been framed love."

I crept up to the wall below the front room window and slowly edged upwards, hoping the plant in the window obscured me. I could see my Mum and Dad, they were hugging each other.

"Oi, nosey git what you looking at?"

I banged my head on the windowsill as I dived for cover.

I looked upwards to see Freddy hanging out of his window. "Cheers" I mumbled.

"The poor sop's been well stitched up. This is gonna mean trouble you know that?" whispered Freddy.

I rubbed my aching head. "I guess so, but what can we do about it?"

"Come up here. I've got something to show you." Freddy said before shutting the window.

I closed my eyes in horror; the thought of Freddy's bedroom always filled me with dread. It was like stepping into a very dark, murky world full of computers and other flash gadgetry. But it wasn't the technology that scared me, no it was something much worse, much darker and that was the stink.

As I reached the top of the stairs I thought, maybe he had decided to clean up his act; maybe he had turned over a new leaf. When I opened the door I knew that there was more chance of hell freezing over than that smelly oik freshening up.

"You sure there ain't no dead animals under your bed?"

Freddy shrugged his shoulders. "Just shut the door and come in."

For a moment it felt like I was shutting the door of a medieval prison cell, it was always far too dark in here.

"Park your rear down here and have a gander at this," he said, pulling a chair up.

"What you got?"

Freddy swung the monitor round so I could see what he was looking at. It was a complicated spreadsheet full of figures and dates, which may as well have been written in hieroglyphics.

"Not your latest stocks and shares portfolio is it?"

"No you thicko," Freddy said impatiently, "it's the books for SWG."

"Spindle's Waste Group? What does it say?" I said, now fully interested.

"As part of the planning permission they have to make their records available to the Council. I've managed to track them down but the point is it doesn't really say anything."

I felt disappointed. "That's a shame. I was hoping it might trip Spindle up in some way."

"No, you cabbage, what I mean is this lot tells you nothing, no volumes of waste going in, none going out, no vehicle movements, zilch."

"And?" I asked realising I sounded as thick as a brick.

Freddy gave me a little slap across the back of my head. "Listen Einstein, the collection of waste and recycling is Spindle's business so therefore within his company's records…"

"He should show how much is going in and how much is going out." I said, finally understanding.

"Bingo, brain of the year, all it really does is confirm what a dodgy creep Harry Spindle is I'll keep looking into this to see if I can find anything that can help Dad."

"Did you hear them arguing before?"

Freddy nodded. "Yeah, does my head in when they do that."

"Do you think he'll be okay?" I asked.

"Yeah, I think so but let's just keep under the radar until it's sorted-agreed?"

"Agreed."

I got up and walked towards the door. "One more thing Freddy?"
"What's that?"

"You sure nothing's curled up and died in here?"

I quickly shut the door behind me, as the sound of a heavy object hitting it could be heard from the other side.

CHAPTER SEVENTEEN

"Nelson, Nelson, come on, time to get up, you won't get any breakfast down at this rate."

My Mum's voice seemed strange, but I guessed that was probably because I was still half asleep and in that confusing place between dreams and reality.

But at least it was Saturday so there would be no lessons at the referral unit, what a bonus.

I washed, cleaned my teeth, didn't bother to comb my hair, and managed to eat three slices of slightly burnt toast, whilst riding my bike on the way to the yard.

The day at the yard was bliss compared to the first day. Tommy Ratson pointed out the timber he wanted moving and where he wanted it moving to. This time he also gave me the pallet trolley, before he departed with the bottle of whisky in his hand, leaving Zombie ogling both Kickstart and me with his one dark eye! Zombie appeared to be merrily chewing the back seat of a 1986 Austin Metro.

The pair of them started yelping again, I'm sure it didn't really mean anything.

"Can I ask you what you're doing Zombie?"
"You mean chewing this seat lad? Trust me the places I've been in this world you get used to living off the land, I've eaten cactus in the desert, chewed grit in the mountains and gargled swamp juice in the everglades. Besides, this seat has some pretty tasty flavours from the scraps dropped by humans over the years."
"Doesn't your master feed you?"

"He only thinks he's my master and yeah he feeds me loads. Besides, it's a hard habit to break. You fancy a taste it's rather splendid?"
"Er, no thanks Zombie just had some dog biscuits."
"Fair enough young 'un."

I continued watching Zombie rip the car seat up and it appeared he was actually eating it!

I shook my head and got on with the task at hand. Using the trolley was a godsend and I quickly managed to fill ten pallets in just over three hours. So I had done more than the work Tommy had set out for me.

I quickly packed up and started to make my way to the mine, dropping Kickstart back at home. Although it seemed like he would be more than happy to stay here at the yard with Zombie, with whom he had got pretty chummy.

CHAPTER EIGHTEEN

As I approached the top of the bank in the town, near the entrance to the woods, there were three police cars, two ambulances and a fire engine parked up. Various uniformed bodies were standing around looking very important and trying to keep the crowd of rubberneckers back from the "crime-scene". There was a small congregation of the town's usual busybodies, who took it upon themselves to stand around and come up with the wildest explanations as to what was actually going on.

"They say there were three bodies?" One middle-aged woman stated, her arms folded beneath her large bosom.

"No, I heard it was one body and two suitcases of cash," a second woman, with an even larger bosom, chirped in.

"Two bodies, three suitcases and six machine guns" and so it went on.

I walked slowly around the back of the crowd and noticed the rosy faced, portly figure of Larkley's finest law enforcement officer – Police Constable Ben Riley. Ben was not exactly, what you might say, up to speed with street gang culture, or about to head the biggest crackdown on organised crime in mainland Europe, but he ran a fairly tight ship in the town, and there was a simple reason for that. Maybe the "good cop, bad cop" approach worked for the forces in inner cities but in our small town, in the dales of Northern England, a much more straightforward approach worked just fine. If PC Riley caught you up to no good, you knew he would you take you straight home where he would leave your folks to deal with you. And most parents in Larkley knew if they didn't deal with their wayward kids Ben Riley would deal with them!

"Now then Nelson, you keeping your nose clean lad?"

"Trying to PC Riley."

"Good to hear to hear it lad, I don't want you ending up in the sewer at your age." He looked me up and down. "You know your problem lad don't you?"

I shrugged my shoulders nonchalantly knowing that resistance was futile.

"Unlike half the wasters round here, you've got some grey bits kicking around in that head and got some good folks back home who'll sort you out."

"I'm keeping it real PC Riley. Honest!"

PC Riley stared at me for a few seconds with an appropriate police-like narrowing of his eyes. "Keep it more than real Nelson and you might just get that keep out of jail card!"

A change of tack was required. "So what's going on?"

PC Riley turned back to the crowd. "Not sure Nelson. Got the call to come down and keep this lot away from a team of Bobbies who are down in the woods, where there was a report of some sort of disturbance."

"Why aren't you down there with CSI?"

"I'm the friendly, daft chump who tries to help people and the one who ends up doing naff jobs like crowd and traffic control."

I felt a bit sorry for him, after all he had always been all right with me and had cut me more than enough slack over the years.

"I see something," one large-bosomed bystander suddenly shrieked.

"It looks like some kind of escaped animal, like a bear, or maybe a gorilla."

PC Riley looked at me and rolled his eyes skywards.

"Right ladies, clear the way and let the officers come through."

PC Riley used his big frame to force the gaggle of rubberneckers to make way.

At the end of the large-bosom lined passageway, beyond the stile, could be seen the slightest of partings into the thick foliage of the woods. And in the middle of that parting could be seen the movement of conifer trees as someone, or something, made its way to the clearing ahead.

A sudden hush came over the crowd and cut the chitchat out instantly. A giant cop stepped to one side and held the trees apart, as two more cops emerged into the daylight dragging a large animal that was kicking and thrashing for its life. The crowd took a collective step back, as the realisation that something quite dangerous was within biting distance.

I crept around the edge of the throng where there was the smallest of gaps and, when I saw whom the coppers were holding down, I recoiled in shock.

His eyes met mine instantly and that was the moment he stopped fighting with the cops. I knew that he had recognised me in that split second, just as I had recognised him- Chucker Wilson; all round nutcase and the best thrower of small human beings in the Northern Hemisphere.

The wild man of Larkley Woods had finally been caught and he looked a mess. He was dragged to his feet but his eyes never left mine. As he was led away and forced into the back of a waiting police van I wondered if some similar, equally as horrible, fate awaited me. I gulped heavily and turned round to see PC Riley looking at me. There was no need for him to tell me what he was thinking; if I didn't clean up my act it would be me getting dragged out of those woods next time.

I would have to try my best to keep my nose clean.

CHAPTER NINETEEN

Sparky threw over one of the helmet lights that Eloise had given him and a large rucksack. "Get those strapped on and follow me."

As we entered the mineshaft I was surprised how quickly the light disappeared. The change from light to blackness was instant and Sparky, being used to how the tunnel changed direction, thought it would be a lark to leave his light off for a moment, leaving me to fumble and stumble in the dark, until I managed to turn my light on. When I finally flicked the light on it was if I was walking into the mouth of a yawning giant and the way the tunnel dipped quickly downwards it felt like we were about to be devoured by the said giant.

"There's some standing water just ahead and it's pretty deep," Sparky warned, as he leapt over a stream in front of him.

"I'll tell you something," I said, as I too leaped, "you've got guts coming down here by yourself."

"Fortune favours the brave and greedy."

I couldn't see his face but I knew Sparky was smiling. He made no bones about his quest to make his fortune. After all, that was the reason we found ourselves walking head first into the freezing blackness down here.

"It gets a bit tricky just here, so watch your step Rabies."

He really was the master of the understatement. "A bit tricky" turned out to be the pair of us edging along a tiny ledge about two metres above a pool of water that looked like it was deeper than anything I cared to fall into.

The ledge was no more than a few centimetres wide and climbed upwards to about three metres above the pool. My fingers suddenly took on superhuman strength, as they gripped the slimy, smooth walls of the tunnel.

We eventually reached the other side only to be confronted by a solid wall with the slightest gap at the foot of it.

"Is this it?" I said in dismay.

"It's not quite the end of the line, watch this."

Sparky dropped to the floor, made himself as flat as possible and started to squeeze through the gap.

The idea of being stuck under a few thousand tonnes of rock that could move downwards at any time and make an instant flat-pack version of me was terrifying. I didn't have the same hunger to make my fortune as Sparky.

"No way, absolutely no way man."

"If you don't you'll never know what's waiting here," Sparky said, from somewhere behind the wall of rock.

Unfortunately, curiosity always gets the better of me; whatever the risks to either my health or increasing the chances of getting into trouble.

The squeeze through the gap was more difficult than I imagined. The rock below me was cold and wet and the rock above me was jagged and sharp. I had to twist and turn my body like some kind of contortionist. At one point I was convinced that I was wedged between the floor and the rock above. My heart came to a screeching halt, as the horrible image of my decaying corpse stuck between a rock sandwich came flooding into my mind. Fortunately Sparky's instructions to relax and breathe normally eventually helped me get out at the other side.

Sparky patted me on the back. "Good show Rabies my son, good show."

"This had better be worth it."

"It is, trust me."

Sparky waited for me to catch my breath before he aimed his torch into the cavern where we now found ourselves. The backdrop was a canvas of green, purple and blue rock, the colours of which, even in the gloom of the cave, danced vividly in the torchlight.

"This, my son is our ticket to a big fat payday."

"It's beautiful," I said, stroking the cool, glassy surface of the fluorspar blocks that formed the cavern wall.

"I've already got a load out using the tools. Mind you, we might have to blast a bit of the rock out next."

"Blasting! You're mental, I'm out of here." I said.

"Oh come on we're mineral miners. We've gotta do some blasting. My Uncle Tommy knows a bloke who blasts in his quarry using black powder. I'm sure we can nab some."

"If you want to put yourself on the Anti Terrorist Squad's most wanted list feel free but count me out." I declared, putting several of the blocks of fluorspar into my rucksack and heading for the gap.

"Where's Nelson Rabies's famous sense of adventure?" Sparky asked, as he loaded up his own rucksack.

"It's locked up with my file at the Unit. I don't mind helping you chip away at a few sparkly rocks but I reckon blowing up a hillside might spoil the chances of my appeal succeeding."

Sparky held up his hands. "It's a fair cop gov. I keep forgetting you're a dead man walking."

"You feel free to either blast yourself to bits, or bury yourself under a thousand tonnes in this place, I'm off."

I started to squeeze myself back through the gap with much more ease than the last time.

Sparky pushed himself through like a man who had done it all his life.

We soon found ourselves standing on the side of the wall I preferred to be on.

"Come on let's get these out of here." I said, as we began the dangerous trek back along the ledge, laden with fluorspar up into daylight.

Once we were out of the mine Sparky and I rode along the track like a couple of motocross stars, making jumps and skidding all the way to the locked gate. We skidded onto the access track, as it started to drop down and felt like a couple of downhill racers, ready to dice with death.

It was only when we were peddling at high speed that I noticed the black 4 x 4 at the bottom of the track.

I whistled at Sparky, indicating to him to stop peddling and we freewheeled for a moment.

Sure enough, there was Cold Eyes, the big, ugly bloke I'd seen with Harry Spindle, as he got out of the 4 x 4 and started to unlock the gate.

Had he seen us? If not we had to hide now; otherwise it would be a case of turning the bikes around and trying to use leg power to outgun his black beast.

"What's up Nelson?"

"I'll tell you in a minute, we just need to hide - and now."

I picked my bike up and dived into the thick undergrowth by the side of the track, leaving Sparky looking on like a bewildered monkey.

"Come on man, get down here quick." I whispered.

"Why, what's up, we ain't broke any laws- well not too many I think!"

I looked down the lane. The 4 x 4 was making its way towards us at a steady pace; steady enough for me to think that maybe Cold Eyes hadn't seen the pair of us yet.

I grabbed Sparky's bike and threw it into the undergrowth.

"Hey, what you doing you........."

Sparky didn't have time to finish his sentence as I threw him in the damp undergrowth next to his bike.

"Just lay low for a minute and then you can rollick me."

Sparky gave me a look which told me he wasn't too happy but at least he had decided to shut up.

I peered through the long grass as the 4 x 4 slowly pulled alongside and, although he didn't actually stop, Cold Eyes looked in our direction. The thickness of the undergrowth meant we were out of view.

As the 4 x 4 drew away I could sense Sparky moving around.

"I'm bleeding soaking now Nelson you pillock."

"Soz, Sparky let's just get the hell out of here."

I got back on my bike and could just see the tail end of the 4 x 4 going over the brow of the hill.

"Where do you get to on that other track Sparky?"

Sparky looked up. "It leads to the old limestone quarry, nothing up there of much interest, apart from a massive big hole and a couple of closed down mine entrances."

As we set off back home I wondered why the stranger with the dead eyes would be visiting an old quarry in the middle of nowhere.

CHAPTER TWENTY

As I sat opposite Miss Steint in the classroom at the referral unit, alongside Mum and Dad, she seemed even larger than I remembered from our last meeting. In fact she had taken on a new look - there was definitely something different about her.

"So I hear good things from Mr Ratson," she said, with a bellow from somewhere deep and dark, "he tells me you are hardworking, punctual and polite."

Mum looked over at Dad. "Are you sure he isn't talking about another Nelson Burns?"

"Oh that would be silly."

I could sense that the only person in the meeting who didn't realise that Mum was joking was my exclusion officer.

"As long as you know the real reasons you are there." Mum said, having recognised that I didn't seem to mind this work lark too much.

"Maybe you can tell us what you have learned about yourself so far Nelson?" Miss Steint asked.

I was trying not to be too distracted by the change that had come about her. Just what was it she had altered?

"Er, that I had er, been pretty stupid."

"Give that man a cigar," Dad said.

"Thank you Billy but I think that maybe, just maybe, Nelson might be starting to see the light." Mum said.

"I agree but there's still a long way to go." Miss Steint declared. "Can I ask you a question Mrs Burns?"

My mother looked taken aback.

"Er, yes of course Miss Steint." Mum stuttered. My Mum seemed to be momentarily off guard, mind you I could understand being intimidated by the browless one…

And then the reason hit me like a thunderbolt, why Miss Steint's appearance had bugged me – she had shaved her eyebrows off! And the reason it was such a shock was because that eyebrow had been the bushiest monobrow I had ever seen. It was like a knitted boa constrictor had been removed from her forehead. I found myself transfixed by her huge, and now bald forehead.

"Do you still run that little environmental group from the youth club?" Miss Steint said, almost without expression, although without the aid of eyebrows it was difficult to fathom her expression.

"Yes, as a matter of fact I do and it is proving popular with lots of the kids. Why do you ask Miss Steint?"

"I just wondered if you did anything for the local moles?" Miss Steint asked excitedly.

Dad looked at me, rolling his eyes in such a manner that I guessed he thought that my referral officer was crazier than the number one crazy person from the crazy hospital. I agreed.

My Mum managed to keep a straight face. "Moles, no, not really. They aren't an endangered species, although I have talked to local farmers about trying to cull them more humanely. Why, are you a keen fan of moles Miss Steint?"

"Oh yes, they are lovely creatures," Miss Steint said a bit too excitedly. "They make their little burrows like cities beneath the ground, only coming up in the middle of the night. When you think about it they are like little soldiers protecting their empires in the dark."

Now it was my Mum's turn to look like she was talking to the winner of Crazy of the Year.

"Er, yes I see what you mean. We haven't any plans for mole projects but if we do…."

"Oh, if you could I would be more than happy to give a lecture on the local species, especially albino moles."

Miss Steint's huge smile threatened to engulf us all. "Now remember young Nelson keep up the good work and don't let your parents down."

As the three of us walked out of the referral unit Dad nudged me.

"I can't decide who should be more worried you or the moles," he said, without the slightest hint of a smile.

CHAPTER TWENTY-ONE

"You ever used an arc welder son?"

"'Fraid not Tommy?" I admitted.

Tommy Ratson took off his ever-present old trilby hat to reveal a fine head of brown curly hair.

"That's a shame, I could've done with someone who could weld a few bits of metal together."

"I'm a quick learner?" I enthused. If I could learn to weld it would be another skill to take into the real world if, in the worst-case scenario, my appeal went belly up.

"It's not that easy you know," he said, squinting at me, before pulling out a bottle from his jacket pocket; although this time instead of the liquid being golden it was clear.

"Fancy a sip?" he offered.

"No thanks Tommy, trying to keep out of trouble these days you know."

"You won't get in trouble drinking this young fella trust me."

I gulped, not wanting to upset him but also not wanting to go anywhere near whatever was in that bottle.

"Relax, it's only water."

I looked at suspiciously. "Water?"

"I guess my reputation goes before me eh?" He laughed, a laugh that echoed around the yard and this time Kickstart scuttled off, straight past Zombie who was running around in a small circle for no apparent reason. "But this really is water. I've got a stream back home and this is pure ground water, fresh as nature itself. I started drinking it the other day and it's kinda addictive, got a real sweet taste."

He offered the water and I took it reluctantly. He was right, it did have a sweet flavour but I quickly handed the bottle back.

"Please yourself. Ok then, back to the welding."

And so Tommy pulled out his ancient looking welding box, helmets, gloves and rods, which would not have looked out of place in some old horror flick laboratory. Tommy dusted the gear off and gave me one of the spare helmets.

"Keep that lid down son. Nought worse than a touch of welder's eye. If you see the light from the welder, stays with you for weeks and it's pure agony."

With that I slammed the lid down and found myself in complete darkness as I looked through the tiny square lens.

Suddenly Tommy sparked the welder into action and I watched the brilliant white light blistering away as Tommy proceeded to weld two car doors together. Ten minutes later and I flicked the lid up to see Tommy standing over a perfectly crafted weld about half a metre in length. The two car doors were welded together in a perfect v shape.

He handed me the welder and an hour or so later, after several moments of melting metal, sticking the rod to the weld and getting a couple of minor shocks as I changed the rods, I started to get the hang of it. I stepped back and admired my work.

"Looks like bird droppings doesn't it," Tommy said, obviously failing to recognise the genius of my handiwork. Mind you, compared to the beautiful lines of his work he was right.

"Keep practising. Here's a few rods and I'll see you in a couple of hours."

As he wandered off I looked at the v shaped metal lump in front of me.

"What are we making here Tommy?"

"You'll see young 'un, you'll see."

And with this he walked away leaving me to weld two car doors together for no apparent reason. Still, it beat Geography.

CHAPTER TWENTY-TWO

My Mum loved to cook for people, and since she was such a flipping good cook, it was nice for others to come round to our place and taste it. The only trouble was it was the whole Hammond clan that she had invited; Sparky, Eloise and their Mum and Dad. I didn't mind, I liked the lot of them but Sparky's big ambitious gob might get the better of him and land both of us in a major cesspool of trouble. And having Eloise around our house only made me feel - well awkward, and it didn't help that everyone knew it!

I had been dispatched to clean the yard and garden, where we were all to sit outside to relax in the glorious evening sun. And as I swept the patio area I failed to notice someone had walked up behind me.

"You really have reached the top Nelson Burns."

I turned around to see Eloise. She did have a talent for sneaking up on me and catching me doing something pretty uncool.

"A clown's gotta do what a clown's gotta do. So how was school today?" I asked.

"Oh the usual. Teachers, PE and homework, no one punching the school bully or anything like that!" Eloise said.

"Bit of a slow day then," I said, not looking up.

"Mind you the circus is not as funny without the main clown."

"Nelson can you get the patio table and chairs out and set them out please," Mum's voice requested from the kitchen.

"She's making you pay big time for your crimes isn't she?" Eloise said.

I looked up. "I guess I deserve it."

Freddy and Sparky walked down the path towards us laughing about some private joke.

"What's up?"

Sparky smiled. "Oh the usual, just discussing markets, shares, the price of explosives."

I looked at them in horror. "Sshh man."

Freddy looked skywards. "Don't suppose the CIA's main satellite is beamed down on the garden of 16 Raleigh Crescent, Larkley is it?"

"What are you lot laughing at?" Mum asked, as she carried a plate of food down the path.

"Trust me, you don't want to know Aunty Lou," said Eloise.

"I'll take your word about that – for now." Mum eyed us all suspiciously but with a twinkle in her eye.

Before long Sparky and Eloise's folks had turned up with wine for Mum and Dad and home made dandelion and burdock for the rest of us. Not quite the preferred drink of your average teenage rebel, I admit, but trust me nothing compares to Mr Hammond's home made dandelion and burdock.

Mum's food was as popular as ever, as was the wine and soon everyone was laughing and enjoying the night. The parents' rubbish jokes surfaced, the slightly drunk but extremely embarrassing Dad dancing appeared, as the music was turned up and daft games commenced.

That was about the time I left the party and went up to my room. I walked into the darkened room, closing the door behind me. I looked through the window and down at the happy faces below and smiled. It was great to see everyone enjoying themselves, especially my Mum and Dad, after everything I had put them through.

And that was when I started to cry. I had hurt them so bad and let them down so much that I felt I didn't deserve to enjoy myself. I sat down on the floor and closed my eyes.

CHAPTER TWENTY-THREE

"Wake up you boghead."

The morning sun blazed through a gap in the curtains as Freddy shook me from my deep slumber.

"What happened to you last night?" he asked, sounding pretty peeved.

"I was feeling a bit dodgy, needed to lie down," I lied.

"You missed a right laugh later on, Dad decided to climb up the top of that wonky old silver birch to see if he could see Harry Spindle's place." Freddy could hardly talk he was so keen to get the words out. "Then he fell backside first into the pond."

"Is he okay?"

"Yeah, a bit wet and a bit embarrassed but apart from that, he'll live."

"So did he see anything?"

"He reckons he saw a lorry leaving, but it was about 11.00. I hacked into Spindle's system and there is no record of it."

"So what do you reckon is going on?" I asked.

"Beats me but who the heck leaves Larkley in a truck at that time of night?"

I raised a knowing eyebrow. "Someone up to no good that's who."

"Anyway Mum says just 'cos it's Sunday you don't get a day off. Get your togs on we're off down Dad's allotment."

I didn't mind. One of Dad's bail conditions was that he didn't go anywhere near his allotment, the allotment club, or anywhere where he might be tempted to start a new green waste empire!

"We're painting the hut apparently. Baggsy I've got the inside," Freddy blurted.

"I know what that means. You get to have a kip while I'm working my peanuts off," I knew what a champion skiver Freddy could be.

"How dare you tarnish my good reputation," he said, with enough made-up hurt in his voice to win an Oscar.

"I tell you what, first there gets to take their pick." Freddy said, already running down the stairs and out of the front door.

Sure enough by the time I reached the allotment Freddy was already in the hut and had closed the door.

If I wasn't in enough trouble I could quite happily have killed my brother there and then.

It seemed eerily quiet and rather deserted until I realised Old Jed was in his allotment as always. But for once he was actually beavering away, like a, well like a beaver I guess.

I couldn't quite make out what he was doing and so hitched myself up on the corrugated iron roof of my Dad's hut. I made quite a noise scrambling upwards.

"Oi, keep it down some of us are trying to sleep," Freddy barked from within.

"Hiya Jed," I shouted but the old fellow didn't hear me.

I was intrigued and so jumped onto the ground and made my way to the adjoining fence.

Jed's side of the fence was about two feet deep in brambles, weeds and grass. I had to poke a hole through the vegetation before I could see in.

Jed had been working the ground and planting something, maybe it was potatoes, or cabbages. I was sure my eyes were playing tricks on me for in the ground was a radio, followed by a toaster, then a kettle. The whole of the allotment was peppered with every small electrical item you could think of.

"A fine crop don't ya think young Nelson?"

The sight of Old Jed's bloodshot, yellowish eyeball peering through the hole, no more than a few centimetres from my own made me yelp and fall backwards.

Jed's craggy face appeared above the brambles. "What's up, never seen a gardener at work?"

"Er, no it's not that it's just..." I spluttered.

Old Jed stuck a rollie in his mouth and lit it. "I gotta admit it ain't ya usual crop is it son but trust me if these grow I'll have a harvest to be proud of."

Jed took a long drag on his fag. "Well that's enough chit-chat, these little beauties won't grow on their own will they."

And he was gone, leaving me sitting in the dirt wondering if it was him or me who was cracking up.

I was starting to get the feeling that Larkley was not the place it used to be. Ever since being booted out of school things had taken on a whole new dimension, as if I had entered a strange, parallel world.

CHAPTER TWENTY-FOUR

I completed painting the outside of the cabin a few hours later in a rather fetching whitewash finish as Freddy finally awoke from his slumber, before he proceeded to do a token twenty minutes of painting and we returned home.

"I saw a Dingy Skipper and a Green Hairstreak today," Mum declared upon returning from the nature reserve.

"They members of a death metal band?"

"Very funny Nelson; actually they are rare butterflies and to get them both down at the nature reserve is a real bonus."

"Only joking Mum, well done." I knew how much it meant to her.

Mum walked over to the sink, as I washed up the pots from Dad's attempt to make a veggie curry.

"Was it as bad as usual?"

I grabbed my throat as I pretended to choke. "Worse, mind you by the time I took the burnt bits out there wasn't a lot left to eat- luckily."

Mum laughed, which in turn made me laugh.

"This feels more like the old days", she said.

I sighed. "I'm sorry Mum."

"Is that why you left the party early last night?"

I nodded and Mum put her arm around me. "I know why you did what you did to that idiot Douglas Spindle but he wasn't worth all the pain was he?"

"Understatement of the century there Mum."

"That boy is going to turn out just like his Father."

"King of the Slugs."

"And that's why both you and your Dad have to keep your noses clean – once you make an enemy of a Spindle – always an enemy. Besides, I'm starting to have a bit more confidence in you- only a little though."

"Cheers Mum," I said, feeling very guilty that I was still helping Sparky pursue his dreams of becoming a gem millionaire. Maybe I should go and see him at the mine and tell him I couldn't afford to keep on helping him. Yep, tomorrow I was finally going to put an end to my stupidity.

Suddenly there was a loud, hard knock at the front door. I wondered who possessed such an official sounding knock as Mum opened the door.

"Well you've got the cheek of the devil I must admit."

I peered around the door to see Harry Spindle standing, large as life, in the frame of the front door. There were a couple of heavies hanging about, further down the path, but they had their backs to the door. It was almost a mirror image of Douglas Spindle and his two hangers-on from the woods the day before.

"Ah, Louise, may I say how gloriously radiant you look this fine evening."

"No, you may not and it's Mrs Burns to you."

"Oh, come come Loui…er, Mrs Burns. Despite the situation with your husband surely we can still be civil."

"Civil, civil? You don't know the meaning of the word you stupid lump of…"

Dad put his hand on Mum's shoulder as he stepped alongside her. "Don't Louise, don't say it because that's what he wants."

"Just why are you here Spindle?" Dad snapped.

"Glad you've got the sense to listen Billy, this won't take a moment." Spindle shuffled uncomfortably. "You see I think we can avoid all this mess, maybe get the charges against you dropped and get all this press about you stealing the green waste sorted out."

"For the record Harry, I never stole your compost." Dad said calmly.

"Well, we could argue about that all night but I if you agree to tell the press what a great employer I am and how concerned for the environment my company is, maybe we can forget the charges."

Dad had obviously had enough of Harry's hogwash because the next thing I knew Spindle was being frogmarched down the path and thrown onto the street.

It was then that my heart missed a beat. For standing there on our path was Cold Eyes, no more than four feet away from me. My lungs felt like they had been filled with anti freeze. Cold Eyes looked at me – a look that perhaps a great white shark might give its prey before biting them in half.

"You're gonna regret this Burns, that was assault- you saw him assault me didn't you?" said Spindle.

Cold Eyes and the other heavy both nodded.

"I'm gonna take you to the cleaners, sue you and get you and your scummy family thrown on the street."

Spindle dusted himself off. "Come on" he barked to his heavies. Cold Eyes stood his ground for a moment before walking away, smiling.

When they had disappeared Dad walked back into the house.

Mum hugged him and then looked straight at him. "If he's serious what are we going to do? We can't afford a decent solicitor – we could lose anything."

"He's bluffing," Dad said, but I could tell he wasn't so sure. If Spindle really did try to sue my folks they would never have the money to fight him. I wondered if there was a way of helping them raise some money. There was a way to help and I knew now I had no choice but to take it.

CHAPTER TWENTY-FIVE

I don't know how he had pulled it off but Sparky had somehow managed to get a huge, old diesel generator up into the mine entrance. The fact that the entrance was set back in the vegetation, growing high up on the quarry face, and the generator looked like it weighed a tonne made it even more baffling and impressive.

"Block and tackle my son, simple physics at work." Sparky replied, as if he had been doing this sort of thing all his life.

"It's a pulley and rope system for lifting heavy objects. Uncle Tommy had one hanging about his yard."

I was still confused. "How did you get the generator here in the first place?"

"Uncle Tommy gave me a lift, said he was coming this way anyway to look for scrap metal."

"Guess he's looking for some scrap to weigh in is he?"

Sparky looked confused. "Actually he said he wanted some old metal for something he was building back at the yard. Normally Uncle Tommy sells scrap as soon as he finds it."

I wondered if it had something to do with whatever we had been welding together.

"So what's the generator for?" I asked.

"Cutting tools and an industrial strength power wash."

Sparky held up the gun-like lance of the power wash in one hand.

"Let me guess - Tommy's yard?"

Sparky nodded. "This power jet is powerful as hell and could take your skin off if you stood in front of it." Sparky looked pleased with himself. "And in the same manner it will clean all the soils and clays off the face of the mine."

"And will reveal what stone's in the wall beneath it." I said, realising his plan.

"Yep, and then we can either cut it out or break it out."

"With what?"

"Actually I got some…"

I raised a hand to stop him in his tracks; I had already guessed where whatever tools he had in his possession had came from. "So what you got?"

Sparky lifted a pneumatic saw, about 20 centimetres long and about the size of a small grinder. "This, old Uncle Tommy assures me, is a diamond saw. He worked abroad for several years, in between his bouts in jail, in some of the roughest and most dangerous mines in the world. And he has had this little baby stashed away ready to use in anger one day."

"I bet he never expected it would be used by his nephew and mate in an old mine in the hills near Larkley."

"Probably not."

"Come on then Sparky. We ain't gonna end up as millionaires just looking at the kit."

Sparky seemed surprised. "You're pretty enthusiastic today matey?"

"Let's just say that Harry Spindle gave me the reason I needed."

"That'll do me. As long as you're up for it."

I grabbed hold of the power wash and lugged it into the mine. It took a while to drag the heavy equipment down the mine, along the ledge, over the rock pool and towards the wall of rock that we had to crawl under.

"So now what do we do?"

Without warning Sparky jumped into gear and started squeezing his way under the rock.

The small light on my helmet hardly lit up the huge cavern and the shadows seem to take on a life of their own. This place was huge, dark and scary.

Suddenly my blood froze as I saw the toothless face of old man looking down from up in the ceiling of the cave.

"Aaahhh." I screamed, but when I looked back, it wasn't a face just a rock.

"What you doing?" Sparky's muffled voice said from the other side of the rock wall.

"Just spooking myself I think." I said, checking the rock again to make sure that it really was just a rock and not a face. But even the rock seemed to have gone. "Just hurry up Sparky can't you."

"Right push the saw, hose and cables through, fire the generator up then bring the power wash lance with you."

I fed the equipment through the gap at the foot of the wall and felt Sparky tugging as he took them through to the cave at the other side. After a few false starts I got the generator working by pulling the old ripcord. I grabbed the jetwash lance and started the awkward scramble under the rock.

My journey was made easier by the light that was pouring in from the cave I was approaching.

"Wow! Did you nick the lights from Wembley or something?" I said, on entering the brilliantly lit cavern. I was impressed; Sparky had rigged up three sets of halogen work lamps, which were powered by the generator.

"Feels a lot different doesn't it?" Sparky said.

"Right get those safety goggles on my son. It's blast off time."

Sparky held the lance, machine-gun like, and aimed it at the wall in front, bracing himself. As he pressed the trigger he was nearly knocked off his feet. That power wash was industrial strength. But Sparky was nothing if not determined and he held his ground as the lance started to blast lumps of clay off the face.

The clay was really thick and stubborn and it took a long time to peel off and fall to the floor. But when it did fall away it revealed a canvas of fluorspar in the rock wall.

"Woohoo." Sparky yelled, as he put the lance down and scrambled up the wall. "I have no idea if this is worth a quid or ten grand but right now it looks mighty pretty to me."

"I agree." I enthused, hoping that I was looking at the way to help my Dad out.

For the next hour or so we soldiered on, exposing the fluorspar, cutting lumps out, washing and piling them up. When the generator finally coughed itself into a fuel-starved halt we decided to take a break. A combination of using the powerwash, hacking the stone out of the cave wall and lumping whatever fluorspar we could find into a pile near the wall finally shattered the pair of us.

When we sat down we both found ourselves coughing.

"I'm knackered." I said, in between gasps for air.

"It's the diesel fumes," Sparky said, removing a bottle of water from a rucksack and taking a large swig of water, "but this place should be ventilated enough, after all those miners worked this place for years."

"You sure?" I said, not entirely convinced.

"Of course," he replied, as he threw the welcome bottle of water over.

We sat there, almost in silence, as we drank the water.

After about twenty minutes Sparky jumped back into life. "I'll go and top the generator up."

And he was gone, under the rock wall in a second. I looked at the pile of fluorspar we had collected and then at the gap under the wall; some of the larger lumps would have to be broken down further if they were to go through the gap, otherwise there was no way they could be taken out. I guessed that was why all this mineral had been left in this place. The gap was so narrow we had enough trouble getting our skinny bodies and tools through it. I could imagine the miners in the old days would have been stocky blokes, who wouldn't have been able to squeeze under the gap, never mind get to the rock.

As I thought about all this I suddenly realised that Sparky had been gone for quite a while.

I bent down and put my ear to the ground - I couldn't hear the generator.

"Sparky? You there matey?" I shouted but there was no reply.

"Sparky? Stop pratting about – you okay?" I waited but again there was nothing.

"I'm gonna kill you if you're messing with me."

I walked over to the rock wall and bent down. But I had to pull away. The gap was full of diesel fumes from the generator and I had taken in a mouth full.

I coughed for several seconds and looked around for a cloth to put over my mouth. I ripped the lower part off one of my shirt sleeves and wrapped it over my mouth. My Mum was going to rollick me but right now that was the least of my problems.

This time when I looked in the gap I didn't cough but my eyes started to sting with the fumes. It took a few seconds for my eyes to adjust but finally I could see Sparky's legs about two or three metres into the gap and he wasn't moving.

I slid into the gap and started to scramble towards Sparky. My breathing was laboured and I was bashing my head and shoulders as I made my way towards him. I was panicking but I had to get to him, I knew he was in trouble. In my rush the rag was pulled away from my mouth and I started to gag. My eyes were streaming and agonisingly painful but I was nearly there. The coughing was becoming uncontrollable and I felt myself slowing down.

I started to retch but I needed to reach Sparky. If I could get to him, maybe I could drag him out to the other side. But I was having trouble keeping my eyes open; not only because of the fumes but also closing them eased the pain. I opened my eyes one more time and saw Sparky's face; it was a strange colour.

CHAPTER TWENTY-SIX

I could feel movement, like a shaking sensation and there was a sound, albeit, far away and muffled. The sound became louder; it was like someone was shouting something.

"Mnkkmpmuumubmhdd"

If I had died I was now in a place where they didn't speak my language.

More shaking. "Mnkk mp muu mubmhdd."

The shaking was really violent now and suddenly I felt a sharp, hard slap being applied to my face.

"WAKE UP YOU BOGHEAD."

Suddenly my eyes were open and brilliant sunshine flooded in and blinded me. I didn't have to look to know it was Sparky who was shaking and slapping me and shouting at the top of his voice.

"You're alive! Thank god. For a minute I thought…"

I managed to sit upright and retched violently. "You thought what? I was a goner?"

Sparky slapped me on the back. "Welcome back my man."

It took a few moments but eventually I managed to finally open my eyes fully and see that the pair of us were now sitting outside the entrance to the mine in the sun.

"You've got a bit more colour in your cheeks than the last time I saw you."

Sparky laughed. "Yep, guess that was a close call. Thanks for getting me out."

"Shouldn't that be the other way round?"

"I think your brain has been fried Nelson Rabies."

I rubbed my eyes. "I think it's you who's frazzled – you must've got me out."

"Nope, I passed out in that crack and woke up here so I can't have."

"Then…"

"Then who did?" Sparky finished the sentence for me. My heart was bouncing and we looked at one another in horror.

"Let's get out of here – quickly," I suggested, as both of us scrambled to our feet and made a mad dash for our bikes. Somehow we had made it out of the mine, after being trapped under several thousand tonnes of rock and about to be gassed into oblivion - how? I didn't want to think about it and I guessed neither of us were willing to hang around to find out.

CHAPTER TWENTY-SEVEN

"Not hungry son?" Dad said, as he looked at me across the dining table.

"Not really, I feel a bit ill to be honest."

Dad looked at Mum. "He looks a nasty shade of blue to me Louise."

Dad looked back at me. "Your eyes look a bit sore?"

"I think some of the dust in the yard got into them."

Dad squinted at me. "What you been up to son?"

"Just been down the yard helping Tommy,"

Dad sighed. "You haven't been doing anything stupid I hope. Let's smell your breath."

"Eh?" I said in horror, as Dad leant over the table.

"It's a simple request, let's smell your breath."

"Billy!" Mum said in equal horror, as Dad grabbed hold of my chin and checked my breath and looked at my face closely.

Dad sat back down. "But I gotta tell you son, you look like death warmed up. What's Tommy being making you do- dig up graves?

Freddy laughed again. "Your dream job eh bro?"

Mum wasn't amused. "Freddy, put a sock in it."

Freddy knew when indeed to put the sock in it, although at times he could fit the whole contents of a sock drawer into his big gob.

"So just what has Tommy got you doing?"

"Welding."

Dad nodded in admiration. "Arc, oxy-acetylene? Mig?"

I had no idea what he was talking about. "Oxy–acetylewhatsitsname - I think?"

"That's a good skill to learn Nelson. If all goes belly up you've got a trade to fall back on."

"So what has he got you welding?" Mum asked.

I cleared my throat, stalling for an answer. "I'm not sure."

Dad chuckled. "Well you must know what it is? You repairing some panels? A car? Making some frames for the timber?"

I thought about all the strange things that happened over the past few days. "Ah, that was what they must be, frames for the timber."

"I reckon you've got yourself a touch of arc eye. You're using a welding mask aren't you?"

Mum looked concerned. "He is doing everything the right way isn't he Nelson?"

"Yeah, yeah he makes me wear the mask, gloves, everything." I felt the need to protect Old Tommy. He had treated me pretty well and I didn't want to get him into trouble.

"He'd better! Otherwise he'll have me to answer to!"

Tommy was a tough, big old unit but I wouldn't bet against my Mum if she decided to take him on.

"Anyway, everyone I have a surprise." Mum cleared her throat. "Our little environmental group have been invited somewhere really interesting."

Dad smirked like a ten year old. "Greenpeace not asking you to raid a Japanese whaling station again are they?"

"Billy I'm being serious. We have been invited to visit the SWG waste recycling centre."

"Harry Spindle's place? Of course you're going to tell him to stick his invitation?" Dad said firmly.

"Actually no," Mum said, defiantly "the whole group are going tomorrow afternoon. I think that we should go and see exactly what they do in that recycling plant. We can't keep on criticising him if we remain in the dark."

"Well good luck but my guess is he'll keep you away from what really goes in there." Dad was barely hiding his obvious distaste for Harry Spindle, "He's definitely on the fiddle and somehow I doubt he'll let you and the kids in that group see how he does it."

"Can I come?" I asked, not really knowing how or why I had volunteered.

"Nelson! That would be a lovely idea. We have to be there at 5 o'clock, so as soon as you are finished at the yard make your way up to the industrial estate." Mum patted me on the arm.

Dad looked at me, "Never volunteer," he suggested, before standing up. "Don't forget that while you're playing nicey, nicey tomorrow he's threatening to make us all homeless,"

Dad opened the door and left the room.

Mum looked at me. "There's an old saying Nelson, 'If you want to defeat your enemy sing his song'." I wondered why she really wanted to visit that recycling plant. I guess that's why I wanted to be there alongside her.

CHAPTER TWENTY-EIGHT

I'd never seen a dog break-dancing before. In fact I had never really seen a dog do any kind of dancing. Although there was the time Kickstart had walked through some wet cement and when attempting to kick off the cement that had stuck to his paws, looked like he might have been line-dancing. But in the middle of Tommy Ratson's yard, Zombie, the three legged, one eyed dog was spinning on his back, waving his three legs in the air and then attempting to roll back onto his three paws.

Even Kickstart was watching with amusement, I doubt he had seen anything like it either.

"You're putting some nice moves down there Zombie."
"Cheers Kickstart, 'scuse me if I don't yak too much, I just feel the need to dance."
"How come?"
"No idea mate, just been feeling a bit light headed and a bit jiggy all day."
"You been eating anything strange, like car seats."
"No, nought out of the ordinary today."
"What about drinks, any of that foul smelling liquid that lies in the puddles round here?"
"Ha, no just some water that the old boy brought down from his big kennel up in the hills."
"Just water!"
"Honest, that's all I've had, anyway enough chit chat I just gotta dance me lad."

Tommy had instructed me to weld five car doors together, in a large wedge-like shape, about four metres in length. At the end of the wedge, on a flat edge he had instructed me to weld five buckets in a row, with buckets going up in size and then repeat the whole exercise to make another wedge with 5 buckets welded to it. I really wanted to know what it was Tommy had me constructing but there had been no sign of him for ages, since he had disappeared into one of the bigger sheds. I could hear him in there; I could tell he was doing some welding himself. I could hear the sizzling sound of the welder. In fact, occasionally I could see a huge shadow cast up high on the ceiling, through the shed window, as it was thrown up by the flashes with each arc. It made Tommy look huge and like some kind of mad professor from an old horror movie.

I was actually enjoying the task and my welding skills had come on leaps and bounds. Instead of streaks of crow-cack, I was starting to produce lines that flowed quite smoothly. I was starting to weld fairly consistently and I was really chuffed.

It was soon time to leave for the tour around Harry Spindle's recycling plant. I had done more work than Tommy had asked me to do, more welding and shifted more wood, mainly because I was enjoying myself so much and now that Sparky and I had agreed that the mine project was to be put on hold I had more time and strength. I also had to drop Kickstart off at home. So it was time to leave the breakdancing king of the dog world and head off.

CHAPTER TWENTY-NINE

I had dropped Kickstart off and was cycling along the riverbank, towards the industrial estate. I was lost in my thoughts when I suddenly felt myself being yanked off my bike and into the bushes by the side of the river. I was dazed and not entirely sure what had happened. I wasn't hurt too badly but my left side was stinging like mad from the nettles I had landed in.

I jumped to my feet and rubbed my side trying to get rid of the burning sensation.

"What's up Burns? Got yourself a nasty sting, oh you poor thing!" I recognised the voice and the fat slug it belonged to. I turned around to see Douglas Spindle grinning more like a village idiot than a Cheshire cat. His two cronies were standing next to him and had similar stupid smiles on their faces.

I looked up to see a length of rope strung across the path, tied between two trees. It was the taut rope that had knocked me off my bike.

"Ah, Douglas. I might've known such a cowardly act would be something to do with you."

"We got it wrong, it was supposed to get you across the neck." he said with a menacing smile on his face. "More damage that way."

I sighed as I looked around and weighed up my options. I recognised this stretch of the riverbank. Dad and some of the other allotment owners had some other gardening stuff going on, such as beehives and rabbit hutches, down here.

Douglas was strutting around like a peacock, albeit a peacock without the normal dazzling colours.

He laughed and looked at his two goons who both laughed dutifully with him.

I wanted to get hold of Douglas and throw him in the river, preferably tied to his two cronies but I was outnumbered and didn't fancy a beating.

"So what do you want from me Douglas? I'm getting a bit bored of this chasing malarkey and I've got stuff to do."

Douglas chuckled slyly. "What stuff?"

"Just stuff. Nowt to do with you."

"What could a sad loser," Douglas made the "L" with his thumb and forefinger on his forehead, something I'd expect from a kid about five years his junior, "like you have to do other than help your loser family in their loser ways."

I clenched both of my fists so hard I felt they would never unlock. I took a deep breath.

"Tell you what I'll give you and Dumb and Dumber," Douglas's two rent-a-bozos looked around to see who I was talking about, "a tug of war with that rope up there?"

Douglas looked at the others and let out a huge laugh. The one thing that Douglas prided himself on, probably the one and only thing he had in his sad little existence, was that he had been the Larkley junior tug of war champion for the past three years.

"You are joking?" he said, almost frothing at the mouth.

"Nope, all of you, best of three."

Douglas rubbed his hands. "I don't need these two, bring it on Burns. If you lose we get to beat you up, if you win we get to beat you up."

"Fair enough but at least give me something if I win." I pleaded.

Douglas rubbed his chin thoughtfully. "Five seconds head start – not that it's gonna happen."

Douglas clicked his fingers and one of his buffoons climbed up to get the rope down. Douglas commanded the other clown to mark two lines on the ground- about ten metres apart.

I had never tried tug of war but my Dad had also once been the junior Larkley champion and he had often told me that Douglas only won because of his bulk. I knew that if I remembered my Dad's tactics I would have a chance of beating Douglas.

"It's gonna be pleasure to drag your sorry behind along this path Burns."

Douglas wrapped the rope around his considerable midriff and then threw the loose end over to me.

"Let their weight advantage become their disadvantage." Yes, those were my Dad's wise words. I wasn't really sure what they meant, so hopefully it would quickly become clear.

Douglas was rocking from side to side, actually licking his lips in anticipation.

I looped the rope around me twice and then looked up.

"Oooof" was all I could say, as the excruciating pain of the rope being squeezed around my stomach ripped the wind out of me.

"What happened to ready, steady, go?" I wheezed.

"Oh. Sorry old chap, I forgot," Douglas sneered, as he once again pulled on the rope, dropping me to my knees and dragging me along the grassy bank and over the mark.

"One nil."

I had to stall for a moment to try and work out some tactics.

"Just give me a moment. You nearly cut me in half there."

Douglas's big grin showed how much he enjoyed hurting people. But I had noticed that there was a bare patch in the grass just behind where Douglas was standing. The grass had not grown on that part of the old ash track, a remnant from when ash used to get dumped on the side of the river from the steel works. This meant that the surface was loose gravel and therefore easy to slip on, especially when someone was putting a lot of force down.

I had to manoeuvre carefully, so that Douglas was not aware of the impending risk. I was going to go forwards and he backwards. I wandered around, giving him the impression I was nervous about restarting but then I saw the gravely patch was about half a metre behind him.

"Ready?" He said, forgetting the "steady" and "go" before yanking me hard. I held my own long enough to be only pulled a few centimetres. This made Douglas furious and as he pulled with all his might, he slipped on the gravel and found himself sliding over his own marker.

"One all," I said, already thinking of what my next move would be.

"Right you two over here. Tie yourselves on," Douglas screamed with sheer fury.

"What you up to?" I shouted.

Douglas looked like a livid gargoyle. "You offered to take all three of us on."

"Yeah but," I started to protest, but then thought about my Dad's words of advice, "Let their weight advantage become their disadvantage."

I waited until they were in position before placing my hand on the rope around my midriff, carefully loosening it as much as I could without being noticed.

"Ready," Douglas slowly said," Steady", he was being generous and I managed to loosen the knot some more, "Goooooooooooooooooooowwwww".

I watched as the three of them pulled, with all their weight and strength, while the rope simply slid from around me. Their combined efforts to drag me off my feet meant that the three of them flew backwards and into the bushes, where my Dad and his mates kept their collection of beehives.

I quickly jumped on my bike and started to peddle along the riverbank. I turned round just in time to see Douglas and his two idiot henchmen jumping into the river, doing their best to avoid several thousand extremely peeved off bees. Douglas pulled himself onto the bank. He was shouting something I couldn't quite hear. He also gave me his best evil stare as I put some distance between the two of us but he just looked like the wet slug he really was.

CHAPTER THIRTY

"Where the hell have you been Nelson Burns?" Mum snapped, her voice full of understandable anger, as she waited outside the gates of the recycling centre.

"What's happened to your shirt? And look at your jeans, what have you been up to?"

I looked at the remains of my shirt and then at my knees. The blue material of my jeans was stained green and brown where Douglas had dragged me through the grass. "I slipped over," I claimed, which was sort of true.

"Never mind. We haven't got time for it now, but we'll sort it out later." Mum looked around to do a headcount on the environmental group that were gathered around her.

I recognised several of the group who were suitably dressed in khaki cargo pants, boots and chunky jumpers. There was Mad Mikey, a tall lad from our school, who had left a couple of years ago. There were many rumours that he had become some sort of rebel, an anarchist. According to the stories he once chained himself to a model of Ronald MacDonald and scaled the local town hall clock to protest against the construction of a bus shelter he didn't like.

Today, he was sporting a yellow Mohawk and a tattoo of a burning spear on his neck. Yep, Mad Mikey was madder than Crazy Carol who also happened to be standing outside the gates. Carol was less of an anarchist and more of your nosey neighbour type, who felt the need to be involved with everyone else's business in Larkley and who would start a protest or environmental movement for the slightest reason.

The group also included Eloise who was talking to Mad Mikey.

"Nelson, come over here a minute." Eloise beckoned. As I walked over Mad Mikey slapped me on the back.

"Ah, Rabies, good man, glad to hear you broke out of the system, you gonna join me when we take the Houses of Parliament down next Wednesday lunchtime?"

I wasn't sure how to respond. "Bit of an ambitious plan that isn't it Mikey?"

"Too much for you Rabies eh?"

Yes of course it was too big a plan for me and besides, I guessed storming Parliament would probably get me into further trouble with Miss Steint.

"Na, I would love to but I'm under house arrest with my folks and you know what my Mum is like."

Mad Mikey and Eloise both looked over at my Mum as she organised the group and they both nodded in agreement.

"Fair point." Mad Mikey conceded. "So how come both you and your Mum, the mortal enemies of the Spindle mafia, are even here today?"

Eloise gestured towards Mum. "This group means a heck of a lot to Auntie Lou, educating the local folk about the environment and how we can care for it and stop abusing it. If she can use this visit to inform us even more, then all the better."

Suddenly a large white van screeched to a halt outside. The door opened and when I saw the first red stiletto stepping onto the ground I knew we were in for an entertaining time.

Jenny Regatta, glamorous starlet of the local TV channel, quickly held up a small vanity mirror and adjusted her expertly constructed hair. She pouted and turned towards our group, who were stood there, as one, open-mouthed.

"TJ, get that camera ready in thirty." Jenny shouted.

Jenny Regatta was the rising star of the local TV channel, which my Mum refused to watch because a certain Harry Spindle owned it. Dad also refused to watch her on TV but he had admitted to me that he thought Jenny Regatta looked flipping hot.

Jenny picked up a mike as she looked initially at me and then at Mad Mikey, who looked like he had just fallen in love.

TJ the cameraman was now standing in front of Jenny and counting down from three with his fingers. At the count of one he raised his thumb and Jenny exploded into life.

"Hello, this is Jenny Regatta, for Northside News outside the gates of Spindle Waste Group's much feted recycling group here in sunny Larkley. As you can see a small, local environmental group have gathered outside the gates of the recycling plant, before they walk through them as guests of Mayor Harry Spindle, chairperson of the Waste Group. These lucky few are the first members of the public to pass through the hallowed gates and we are here today to hopefully speak to a few of those lucky people."

Jenny Regatta headed our way and stuck the microphone in Mad Mikey's face.

"Hello," Jenny stuttered, as she was confronted with Larkley's most scary looking eco-warrior, "Could you tell me what you expect from your visit today?"

For the first time since I had known him Mad Mikey was speechless and Jenny looked around impatiently, hoping to find another, more camera friendly, face.

"Would you like to go to the cinema?"

Jenny turned in shock upon hearing Mad Mikey's question. "Sorry?"

"They're showing "Kung Fu Panda." It's my favourite and I thought maybe you'd like to go?"

"Well, er, although it's a lovely idea I really am far too busy." Jenny said before moving on quickly.

Jenny locked onto Eloise. "So young lady what about you? What are you hoping to get from this tour?"

"I'm hoping to see how these aerobic digesters work, especially how they maintain the critical optimum temperature required throughout the decomposing process which should, and I emphasise the should bit, enable the organic matter to be broken down and decomposed into appropriate compost-like material."

Eloise looked at Jenny completely straight faced. She might have been only thirteen but she had a wise old noggin on her shoulders.

"Right, yes, well, er, yes thanks for that."

Jenny was definitely not having the best of times and when the gates opened I think she was relieved to see the smiling face of one Harold Spindle.

"Ladies and Gentlemen, boys and girls, welcome, welcome to SWG, Spindle's Waste Group."

It seemed like Harry was trying to be the Willy Wonka of the recycling world, and it also seemed a little bit creepy.

"Today, you are the first members of the public to be invited into my world, the world of modern recycling technology."

Eloise leaned over, "I think he's going for this year's Oscar for Best Actor."

"Today you are privileged to see the cutting edge of modern technology making this world a better place for us all to live in."

I leaned over to Eloise. "Make that the Nobel Peace Prize."

"Now if you would like to follow me?" Harry stepped to one side and gestured with a raised arm.

As we walked through the gates I somehow doubted that, unlike Mr Wonka, Harry was going to provide us with a glass elevator or rivers of chocolate!

CHAPTER THIRTY-ONE

The first port of call was an area called the "Transfer Station" where several bin lorries were lining up to deposit their loads.

Our group had been kitted out with bright green high visibility vests, yellow hard hats, gloves, protective goggles and steel toe capped work boots.

"Hey Nelson what you doing here?"

I looked up to see Big Lol hanging out of the window of his bin lorry.

"On the Royal tour, Lol."

Big Lol gestured to the group, led by Harry.

"Not quite a red carpet is it?"

I followed his gaze to look into the vastness of the dank, concrete building. We were standing on top of a huge platform, from which another bin wagon was depositing its contents into the expanse below. There was a sea of black bin bags, some of which remained intact, while others had split to reveal the putrid and reeking contents within.

Harry beckoned us all forward to the edge of the platform. On the floor below was what I could only describe as an ocean of waste food, paint pots, mattresses, an ironing board, a cuddly toy bear, smashed furniture, split footballs, broken toys, and oddly enough, what looked like the remains of brightly coloured motorised wheelchair with an "On Tour" sticker on the windshield!

At the far end of the transfer station a huge yellow machine was picking up massive clumps of the rubbish, using a claw on the end of an extended arm, and dropping it down a huge steel chute.

"This, folks, is what happens to your everyday rubbish once our lads in the wagons take your bins away and, as you can see from the sheer amount, there is a great need for recycling."

"And all for the sake of the environment Mayor?"

"Of course Mrs Burns," Harry directed at my Mum, trying to remain calm. He sighed before continuing. "You've seen the "dirty" front end of the recycling process let's move to the next stage shall we?"

Harry Spindle gestured for us to move on.

"Don't fall on the conveyor belt Nelson, don't want ya doing a Veruca Salt do we." Big Lol said, with a wink and a smile.

We were herded along a bright green corridor, which had a strong, fresh smell about it; maybe it was true what they say about the Queen always smelling fresh paint wherever she went on an official visit. We entered the next part of the building that was even more enormous. It contained two huge steel towers, which were connected to one another by a series of conveyor belts.

The floor of the building was a hive of activity with workers scurrying about, forklift trucks being driven around and one or two more official looking men in suits under their green vests not doing much at all.

As we all gathered next to one of the huge steel towers Eloise touched its side.

"It's hot?" Eloise said, holding her hand against the metal of the tower.

"Well, the waste is placed inside these towers at a temperature of 70 degrees Celsius for a specific time, which allows the material to be broken down from the household waste we all throw away into compost material suitable for all your Dads' allotments," explained Harry rather smugly.

"It seems too good to be true to me Harry." Mum chirped in, delivering a nice little punch to Harry Spindle's polished tour.

"In what way Mrs Burns?" Harry replied, appearing slightly rattled.

"Well how can you take tonnes and tonnes of plastic, metal, wood and other stuff and make an organic material to grow vegetables in –it's like alchemy but for rubbish rather than gold."

Crazy Carol leaned over. "What's alchemy?"

"The mysterious art of making gold from base metals." Eloise told her without missing a beat.

Harry put his hands up as if to calm Mum down. "No it's much simpler than that. The metal, plastic and other rubbish that won't decompose are removed before the remaining rubbish enters the towers. There's no mystery to this process. Let's walk up to the gantry at the top of this tower and we'll soon find out how."

The group walked up the six flights of stairs that led to the metal platform at the top of the tower. From the top the full size of the plant could be seen and it was like looking down onto a small city, with the workers on the floor looking like ants from way up here. Conveyor belts swept under housings from which other, smaller conveyor belts sprouted. These smaller belts led to skips, into which the metals were spat. Along the rest of the belts were small groups of workers who watched the rubbish as it swept along, removing any rogue bits of rubbish that didn't belong in the process.

"Now if we walk back down we will see the end result of this amazing technical process. Follow me." I was nearly swept away by Harry Spindle's enthusiasm; he was so keen to show us his system.

As he reached a huge yellow skip at the end of one of the conveyor belts Harry quickly leaned against it, wiping his brow with a handkerchief. Emblazoned on the skip was a SWG emblem, which consisted of a hedgehog, wearing a hardhat, holding a crushed can in one paw and a bottle in the other.

Harry pointed into the skip. "Anyway if you all gather over here and look in this skip you will see what is produced at the end of the process."

Mum peered into the skip. "Is that it?"

"What do you mean?" Harry said defensively.

"I mean you've got all that rubbish being processed by those huge towers and all you have at the end is a skip full of this stuff?"

Harry beamed triumphantly. "Yes, that's all we end up with. " Harry hesitated. "It's kind of like the human body eating lots of food and only having a small poo at the end of the week."

Eloise and I looked at one another knowingly.

"Well that wouldn't be very healthy would it?" Mum suggested sternly.

I could see Harry was becoming frustrated as he tried his best to joust with Mum.

"Well by the time we've segregated the glass, wood, plastic, cardboard and metal and then baked the leftovers in the towers this is what we end up with - compost."

"Is it underneath that fluffy stuff?" My Mum asked, cheekily, knowing the answer already.

"No, that fluffy stuff, as you call it Mrs Burns, is the compost product," Harry said patronisingly.

Mum looked down and studied the contents of the skip carefully. "When you say product, what exactly can it be used for? Because from here it looks like something you would use to stuff a mattress and not much else."

"Instead of Mayor Swindle using ten and twenty quid notes to stuff his own mattress," Eloise whispered.

Harry shook his head, smiling his plastic smile. "This my dear," Harry put his hand deep into the fluffy stuff, "is a fine compost-like material. I have arranged for you all to take a few bags of this material home with you once the tour is over."

"Have you tested it? What is the organic content, if any?" Eloise asked.

"Yes, this stuff has been tested by our own specialists and it has proved to be an excellent growing medium."

"Could we see a report that proves that?" Eloise asked.

"Of course, young lady. Er, when it is produced in a few weeks."

Mum stepped forward. "I'm sure it'll make interesting reading but, until it is published, we will decline your kind offer for those bags of," Mum raised two hands and moved two fingers up and down on each one as if to indicate inverted commas, "compost."

Harry looked dejected. "Okay Mrs Burns but feel free to ring me anytime."

"Don't hold your breath Harry." I whispered to Eloise.

As Harry continued to talk about how good his compost was I looked around the huge building. It truly was colossal and the twin towers loomed over everyone like massive robots, about to vaporise us all. I wandered a few metres away from the group to have a closer look. When I walked up to one of the towers I could see that, although they were pretty tall, their height was increased because they were sitting on huge steel bases. I guessed they contained the electrics, or gas, or whatever was needed to run them. I was just about to walk back to the group when a door, set down in a footwell at the base of the tower, opened and someone stepped out, someone I recognised immediately and it was not a welcome sight.

Cold Eyes looked around the building before locking the door at the base of the tower. He whistled as he put the keys in the pocket of his leather jacket and walked up the stairs, onto the floor. He glanced over at the group. I shrank back into the middle, trying to be inconspicuous.

Cold Eyes carried on walking and went through a door. I was relieved to see the door closing behind him.

"What's wrong with you?" Eloise asked, nudging me in the ribs.

"Nothing."

"Yeah! Looks like nothing. You seen a ghost?"

"I wish." I said.

I looked at the towers, sitting upon the huge steel boxes and wondered what was really under there.

"Well that about wraps up today's tour. Does anyone have any ques…"

Harry was stopped in mid sentence as a loud, shrill alarm sounded somewhere high up in the building. Several red lights started spinning above the doors.

Harry looked alarmed. "Oh, er, there wasn't supposed to be a drill today." He looked around the building, as the workers started leaving their work places and headed for the emergency exits.

Harry, the apparent guardian of our safety, remained rooted to the spot.

Mum looked around the group quickly. "Are we all here? Good then let's get out of here." She started moving quickly towards the exit. "I don't know about you Mayor but we're going outside."

Harry gulped and quickly joined the group.

Outside we gathered inside a green square painted on the floor, near the offices, as Mum did a head count.

Jenny Regatta was standing outside the gates ordering TJ to keep his camera rolling.

Harry talked angrily to two men near the offices, gesturing wildly with his arms and looking rather red in the face.

"Oh heck, we're one short." Mum said, quickly doing a recount, as the rest of the group looked around to see who was missing.

Harry made his way back to the group. "Right, I need you all to leave the premises as quickly and quietly as possible."

Mum shook her head.

"We're one short. There were thirteen of us when we came in and now there's only twelve."

I noticed Jenny Regatta from the corner of my eye, ordering TJ to point his camera towards the roof of the building. I looked up, as did Mum.

"Harry I think I know where number thirteen is."

As Mum pointed upwards Harry slowly followed her direction.

On the roof of the building holding a banner with the words "Proper Compost for Larkley" written across it was a giant hedgehog!

CHAPTER THIRTY-TWO

PC Ben Riley scratched his head vigorously.

"So you sure you knew nothing about this Louise?"

Mum had her arms folded in front of her and looked PC Riley straight in the face.

"Just who do you think I am Ben? The mastermind behind some plot to bring Harry Spindle down?"

"Of course not Louise. But we need to know that loopy goon up there didn't plan this with anyone else."

Mum, PC Riley and Eloise all looked out of the window of the recycling plant's office, to which we had retired following Mad Mikey's protest. Sure enough we could see the hedgehog sitting, quite contentedly, on the roof of the building.

"Ben. You've known Mikey as long as I have. You of all people should know what he's like."

PC Riley nodded gently. "Aye, the lad's brain is often on holiday."

"Well his heart's in the right place." Mum said defensively.

"Of that I've no doubt," PC Riley sighed, "he's protested against everything from trees being pulled down to a pond full of frogs being destroyed."

"Newts, Ben, Great Crested Newts."

"Well, whatever they were, it's all fine and dandy to go round trying to save the world but you can't go dancing around on top of any old building."

"Dressed as a giant hedgehog." Eloise said, trying not to laugh.

"This is serious young Eloise," Ben Riley said, although it seemed like he was trying not to laugh himself.

"Look's like something's happening." I said, as the four of us looked out of the window. A fire engine extended its ladder up onto the roof of the recycling building. Two uniformed police officers stepped across the few centimetres between the top of the ladder and the roof and carefully made their way over to the giant hedgehog. Mad Mikey slowly rolled his "Proper Compost for Larkley" banner up and the cops led him to where the ladder was waiting.

Before he started descending the ladder Mad Mikey was greeted by several cheers from the small crowd that had gathered outside the gates of the recycling centre. Mad Mikey waved a hand, well a paw, in victory and started to climb down the ladder.

"What does he mean proper compost for Larkley?" PC Riley asked.

"I think that young Michael doesn't believe that this place is creating a product that any person in their right mind would put on their garden?" Mum declared.

PC Riley raised an eyebrow as if he agreed. What interested me more was why Cold Eyes was working for Harry Spindle. What was underneath the towers in those huge, metal boxes and just how did the recycling plant manage to reduce thousands of tonnes of household rubbish into a few skips full of "fluff"?"

CHAPTER THIRTY-THREE

When we got home the four of us sat down in front of the TV. The local news was just coming to the end of a story about an Alpaca that had escaped from a nearby farm. Jenny Regatta was listening to her male colleague, as he wrapped up the story; the type of story he always finished with a terrible pun.

"And the good news is that Alan the Alpaca has now been returned to his rightful owners on the farm, although the next time Alan decides to get in the back of a lorry on the way to Edinburgh I suspect his owners will send Al packing."

Jenny Regatta cringed visibly. "I guess that new career as a comedian is still on hold Mike."

"Crikey, that Jenny Regatta is a good looking girl," Mum said.

"Can't say I've noticed." Dad said, giving me a knowing look.

"You don't say." Mum said flatly, and then she also gave me a knowing look.

"Today, the town of Larkley witnessed what could probably be regarded as one of the strangest events in its history."

I wasn't sure that I agreed with Jenny, what with everything that had happened round these parts recently.

"In the tradition of Northside News's high standards of cutting edge journalism I was on the scene as the following report shows."

"Cutting edge journalism? Yep, I bet the BBC and Sky were really cheesed off they never got that Alpaca scoop first," Dad said mockingly.

"Ssshhh." Mum said, as the image of Jenny Regatta standing in front of the recycling plant appeared on screen.

"We're here today right outside Spindle Waste Group's huge, modern and super efficient recycling plant in Larkley. This plant is responsible for producing some of the UK's highest recycling figures. This has helped put Larkley at the top of the national league table for reducing the volume of our household rubbish, into either recyclable products, or good quality compost."

Dad shook his head in disbelief.

"The head of SWG, Mayor Harry Spindle, decided to take those rumours head on and, today, invited a local group of environmentalists to tour the plant."

I looked over at Mum who remained emotionless.

"However, at some point during that tour it would appear that one of the group broke away and decided to hold a one man, or is that a one mammal protest. And we can see that protest in progress right now."

The camera panned out to show the main building of the plant, where a certain huge hedgehog was holding up a banner for all the world to see.

"So much for showing it how it really happened." Mum said, as the words on the banner were pixelated so that they could not be read.

"Unfortunately, due to legal reasons, we cannot show just what the protestor's banner actually said."

"Legal reasons, my elbow, more like Harry Spindle phoned the head of the news channel and told him not to show it." Dad said, through gritted teeth.

The image of Mad Mikey, with the head of his costume removed, being led away by two officers, made strange viewing. The most bizarre thing was that, although Mad Mikey's face had been blurred out, so he could not be recognised, his bright yellow Mohawk and the tattoo of the burning spear on his neck were clearly visible. If he appeared in a police line up, even with his face blurred out, I suspect he would be clocked pretty quickly.

"So now it's business as usual, back here at the SWG recycling plant, where the company continues to strive to maintain its high standards and be a leader in the world of recycling."

I looked over at Mum who was visibly seething as she spoke. "I was angry at Mikey for pulling that stunt but now I admire him. Sadly I feel that his valiant effort may have been in vain."

Mum looked really upset and left the room. Dad looked at both Freddy and me and gestured with his hands for us to stay seated before he followed Mum.

"Adults eh, I still don't get 'em and I'm nearly one myself." Freddy said, before picking up the remote control. He pointed the remote at the screen and started to surf the channels when, suddenly, I saw something about local beauty spots that caught my attention.

"Go back a couple of channels will you."

Freddy sighed impatiently before returning to the channel that was showing some of Larkley's lesser-known beauty spots.

"Where's that?"

"Water Mill Cottages."

"Never heard of 'em."

Freddy smiled. "Don't you remember Mum and Dad taking us there when we were just little kids? Playing in the stream near the old water wheel?"

"Is that the time you got your trunks ripped off by a tree branch and had to come out covering your crown jewels?"

"Yeah, yeah," Freddy said, with the slightest hint of embarrassment showing. "Anyway there was a row of houses next to the old Mill. In fact your present employer is one of the residents up there."

"Tommy Ratson?"

"Yep, and I'm sure a couple of Dad's mates live up there as well." Freddy said, as he returned to surfing the TV channels.

I suddenly had a gut feeling. "Freddy, which one of Dad's mates lives up at Water Mill Cottages?"

Freddy waved his hand at me in frustration. "Oh, er, the old geezer in the allotment next to Dad's."

"Old Jed?" I asked excitedly.

"Yeah, that's the old goat."

That meant that two of the town's more deranged characters lived in the same little hamlet. I suddenly suspected that Water Mill Cottages had something to do with all the strange things going on round here and that they would have to be visited as soon as possible.

CHAPTER THIRTY-FOUR

The next morning I jumped out of bed, mainly because I was keen to get up to Water Mill Cottages later in the day. It was going to take a momentous effort to get up there because before that I had to finish whatever strange tasks Tommy would assign me at the yard.

I had looked on a map and the cottages were about three miles out of the town. I reckoned if I could crack on at the yard, I would have roughly two hours maximum to get up to the cottages and back. Hopefully, Tommy would just have me shifting some pallets of timber about.

That hope was dashed when Kickstart and I arrived at the yard. For the first time since I had started working there Tommy was waiting for me.

"Hurry up son we really need to crack on today."

"You got an urgent job on Tommy?"

My pushbike had hardly touched the floor before Tommy was leading me by the arm.

"Aye, a job alright. A bleeding big one at that."

Kickstart was trotting alongside us and appeared to be struggling to keep up the pace. Tommy was certainly on some sort of mission.

"I got some heavy grade work for you today but don't worry I've got you some help."

"Help?" I asked in surprise.

As we turned the corner, past a leaning tower of burnt out car shells, I saw just who the help was.

"Nelson Rabies, me old mucker, nice of you to turn up."

"I should have known." I said, upon seeing Sparky.

"Don't tell me you were hoping for a more glamorous assistant, like Eloise for example?" Sparky said.

"The grim reaper would've been better." I replied.

"Lads, come over here for a moment." Tommy barked.

I looked at Sparky, who shrugged his shoulders. Tommy stopped in front of a heap of old lampposts. They were originally green but the paint was starting to peel away to reveal bare brown metal below.

"I'd like you two to weld two of these together."

I scratched my head. "Side by side?"

Tommy looked at the lampposts for a moment, absent-mindedly scratching his chin. "No, end to end but I want them to bend at the joint, maybe an angle of about thirty degrees. And there's another two to weld in exactly the same way."

"Daft question of the year Unc, but why?"

Tommy looked at his nephew as if he had just asked if the world was really round.

"One day you'll know." Tommy said, as he turned on his hobnail heels and headed off towards the large building, where he had spent many a recent hour welding.

Sparky watched him disappear. "That is one crazy old codger."

"That's a laugh coming from you. You're madder than a bunch of mad monks stuck on Mad Island where everything you drink and eat makes you even madder."

"Really, thanks very much." Sparky said.

"That wasn't a compliment. Anyway you look better than the last time I saw you at the mine."

Sparky shrugged his shoulders. "I was feeling rough for the first couple of days but now I'm nearly back up to speed and raring to go."

I looked at the four lampposts that Tommy had placed on the floor in two parallel lines. "You any ideas?"

"Absolutely none. It's just another one of his hair-brained schemes. Mind you this seems to be the craziest for a long time."

"Is he building something?" I asked.

"Maybe a spaceship to take him to his home planet." Sparky quipped.

"At least this keeps you away from the mine." I said with some relief. "I forgot to tell you. Just before I passed out I saw the mother of all pieces of fluorspar." Sparky enthused.

The alarm bells started going off in my head. "No way Sparky. No way are you going back for it, just find another way to get rich and in the meantime take Tommy's wage."

Sparky thought for a minute. "Yeah, I guess you're right."

So that was it. We took turns to weld the lampposts together. It was hard going and the welds had to be extra strong but by mid afternoon we had two sets of welded lampposts.

I lifted my welding mask up and admired our work.

"Time for some grub methinks," Sparky said, as he sat down on a crushed beer keg.

As we ate our lunch I noticed that Zombie had appeared and was playing happily with Kickstart.

"No breakdancing today then Zombie?" I said and right on cue, Zombie stared running towards a 1997 Ford Escort and ran head first into the passenger door.

"Ow," Sparky and I said in unison. Even Kickstart seemed to wince.

"You fancy a go young Kickstart?"
"Er, no thanks Zombie, looks a bit too rough for the likes of me."
"I'm not exactly sure why I'm doing this but it sure is fun."
"Don't hurt yourself dog."
"Ol' Zombie doesn't feel much pain these days, not since I had that fight in the Arizona desert with a giant scorpion that scored a direct hit on my chest."
"And you survived?"
"Had to chew the poison out myself but it left me with a niggling pain in my chest and shoulders. Got up this morning and just thought this would help me get rid of the old few aches and pains."
"You been drinking that dodgy water again?"
"Yep, and it makes me feel like a young pup, sure you don't fancy a go?"
"No thanks Zombie you carry on mate."

"Look he's left a Zombie shaped dent in the door." Sparky said, between fits of laughter.

"Don't you think he's getting crazier, like your Uncle Tommy?"

"Maybe but I guess he also drinks or eats the same stuff as the mad monks on Mad Island you were on about before."

"Aye, you're probably right…" Then a thought struck me like a lightning bolt.

"Say that again Sparky."

"Mad monks on Mad Island?" Sparky said in bewilderment.

"No, the bit about him drinking and eating the same stuff."

"Well I guess that's probably true after all Zombie goes home with Uncle Tommy on a night."

"I thought he was the guard dog here at the yard?"

Sparky chuckled. "That's what Uncle Tommy tells everyone but he's far too soft and loves Zombie too much to leave him here. Everyone thinks Zombie is roaming around here but Uncle Tommy just leaves a recording of him barking that comes on occasionally during the night."

"So the two of them eat and drink the same stuff?" I asked excitedly.

"Guess so," Sparky conceded.

"You fancy a ride up to Water Mill Cottages on the bikes?" I asked.

Sparky burped the noisiest burp I'd ever heard.

"Yeah, sure, but I'll tell you now there's not a lot up there apart from a few old cottages, the old water mill and a few grubby old streams."

"I just have the feeling that something up there may be the key to all this madness round here." I said.

"What madness?" Sparky asked.

Zombie suddenly gathered a turn of speed and proceeded to ram himself into the rear end of a 1989 Vauxhall Astra.

"Okay you win," Sparky said.

CHAPTER THIRTY-FIVE

We rode our bikes up the winding path that cut through a thick pine forest before we found ourselves in a clearing. It was fairly dark, with only the odd ray of sunshine breaking through the thick covering of trees but I could see the tumble down water mill up ahead. We continued to ride slowly up the path and it began to become really spooky.

I could see that the water mill was nothing but a shell and its once mighty wheel was now a rotting wooden carcass, covered by thick moss.

I could see a stream cutting its way through protruding rocks behind the mill, which fed into a large, still, dark pond.

"This place is creepy as hell!" I declared.

"Yep, never did work out why Uncle Tommy decided to live up here but I suspect it was probably cheap."

I looked around. "So where does he live?"

Sparky gestured for me to follow him. He rode up a small track, into another clearing, where a row of about five or six tiny cottages were to be found.

"Welcome to Water Mill Cottages, once home to the mill workers, now home to the likes of Uncle Tommy and Old Jed."

"You know anyone else who lives up here?" I asked.

"The only one I can think of is the old crow who is trying to sort you out."

"Miss Steint?" I gasped.

"Yeah, that's the old boot."

Surely, it must have been a coincidence that Miss Steint lived in the same little street as Old Jed and Tommy Ratson but what were the chances of that?

We pulled up in front of one the cottages.

"This is the one she lives in I think."

But Sparky did not have to tell me that Miss Steint lived here; there were dozens and dozens of clues that told me so.

Sparky shook his head as he looked around the neat little garden in front of the house. "Guess she has a thing for moles eh!"

"You could say that," I said, surveying the army of ornamental moles that were crammed across the garden. The first thing that struck me was that they were all painted white.

"Don't suppose she performs some kind of mole voodoo vibe do you?"

"Who knows Sparky but let's leave before she turns up."

Sparky slapped me on the back. "You know what Nelson Rabies I couldn't agree more."

I was about get on my bike when I noticed the small stream that flowed through the front garden of each of the cottages. As the stream made its way through Miss Steint's garden it flowed under a little brick bridge that was guarded by two white plastic moles!

"What's with the little stream?"

Sparky looked into the gardens. "Oh that's the old stream that Uncle Tommy swears by. Reckons it's the best drinking water in England."

"Really?" I said, dismounting my bike and opening my rucksack.

"Come on Nelson. Let's shoot before one of the local loons turn up."

I pulled out my plastic drinking container and flipped off the lid. "Just gotta wash this out."

I opened the gate to Miss Steint's garden that was guarded by, of course, a white mole. I knelt on the grass and dipped the container in the cool water, filled it up and clipped the lid firmly down.

"Okay, we can go now."

"Good idea, I think the place is already turning you into a fruitloop."

I was about to walk through the garden gate when a familiar booming voice stopped me in my tracks.

"Ah, young Mr Burns and what brings you to my humble abode?"

I turned around and immediately I wished I hadn't. Miss Steint was standing there in a bathrobe. Now I was really scared.

"Oh, me and Sparky decided to come up for a ride. He told me how beautiful it was up here." I was blagging; it was the creepiest place on earth.

"Oh thanks, "Miss Steint beamed with pride, "it is a special little place and I noticed you like our very own source of magical water."

"Magical?"

"Well that little stream comes all the way down from the hills, past the old mines and it is the source of lots of natural minerals- keeps us all young and healthy up here. Take as much as you want Nelson."

"Oh this is more than enough, thanks, "I said, holding up the plastic container.

"And do you like my collection of moles?" She said, gesturing to the assortment of awful, eerie models.

"Oh, they're nice Miss Steint, real nice." There was only so much bluffing I could do.

Miss Steint bent down to pick up one of the moles and I suddenly realised she was wearing a wig. But she had a full head of hair last time I saw her, only a couple of days ago, although she had been minus a couple of eyebrows! Was the poor woman ill?

"Do you like moles Nelson?"

"Er, yeah sure – who doesn't?" I stammered.

"Yes of course, but it is the albino mole I really love and want to protect," she said, holding up one of the white models.

I wasn't looking at the mole but at the acrylic monstrosity upon her head, which looked anything but real.

I knew my mouth was open but struggled to speak. "I really have to get home now Miss Steint. Curfew and all that," I eventually managed to say.

"Well we wouldn't want you getting in trouble now would we Nelson, so off you go, straight home."

I smiled and started to ride away. One thing was for sure, Sparky had been right about this place and I began to peddle like a demon.

CHAPTER THIRTY-SIX

"So where did you get this from?" Mum said, holding my drink container up to the sunlight that was streaming through the open French doors that led to the garden.

"Water Mill Cottages," I said, suddenly realising my mistake. "But Sparky got it not me."

Mum looked at me for several long moments. "You sure Nelson?"

"Scouts honour," I said, raising my fingers to my head in a scout-like salute.

"First thing, you weren't a scout and, secondly, if I find out you have been somewhere without telling me, well do you know what a eunuch is?"

I gulped, fully aware of what her threat meant.

"So where did Sparky," Mum shot me a suspicious look, "get this from?"

"A stream near the cottages. He reckons that there is something wrong with the water and it's making everyone a bit weird."

"Weird?"

"Just feeling funny and doing strange things."

Mum studied the water sample for a few more moments. "Okay. Someone at the University labs helps out with our little environment group, so I'll ask them to have a look."

"Cheers Mum," I said, hoping I had been let off the hook.

I walked through the open doors and started to walk along the path.

"Oh and Nelson."

I turned around slowly.

"Don't treat me like a fool."

I quickly scurried off down the path, feeling like I was walking on very thin ice.

Further down the path I came across Dad, who was sitting on a deck chair in the garden with a legal book open on his lap.

"You sure you're doing the right thing Dad – defending yourself?"

He studied me for a moment. "You remind me of myself when I was your age son. When I played guitar with Burnin' Bridges there was many a time we used to run up against authority."

"By the way Dad I listened to that tape again the other night."

Dad's face showed the slightest flicker of pride.

"What the one from Larkley Youth Club? We supported Flux of Pink Indians that night?"

"Who?"

Dad grinned, even now he had an air of rebellion about him.

"You're still an old punk at heart." I said.

"Well hopefully this old punk can expose Harry Spindle as the fraud he is and get myself off the hook." Dad declared. "Don't worry it will all come together in the end, just like life really."

I knew that Dad was upping his chances, as much for himself as for me. The thing is I knew that I would have to give him some sort of helping hand just to be sure.

CHAPTER THIRTY-SEVEN

I'd now made my mind up and there was no going back. I looked at myself in the mirror; decked out in black boots, black jeans and black hoodie. Even my rucksack was black canvas. For a fleeting moment I thought I looked like some kind of Ninja Warrior but then, in reality, I knew I probably looked more like some sad, lonely Goth!

I sneaked down the stairs, making sure Mum and Dad didn't hear me. Kickstart was asleep in his basket and didn't even bat an eyelid- he was officially the world's worst guard dog but tonight I didn't mind.

I carried my pushbike out onto the street and didn't start peddling until I was out of earshot of the house.

I had the wind behind me and I was soon at my first port of call- Tommy's yard. It all seemed quiet; it was past midnight and there was no sign of Zombie. The story about Tommy taking him home must have been true. It was only when I was half way over the fence, that the sound of loud, chilling barking kicked off.

When nothing happened after about thirty seconds I pulled a small piece of fluorspar from my pocket and threw it into the middle of the yard. It made a small pinging noise as it bounced off something. If Zombie was on the prowl it would be enough to alert him.

After a few moments nothing had stirred so I made my way to the tool shed - the reason I was here in the first place. I had a spare key since Tommy had, more or less, left me to my own devices. I unlocked the heavy-duty padlock and opened the door. Inside there were various tools that would be handy for my plan tonight. I wasn't sure why Tommy Ratson had an old rope and grappling iron but I figured it probably had something to do with what Sparky had told me about his dodgy past. Whilst I was scrambling around in the shed I also found some wirecutters that might be useful. Unfortunately, I was fairly sure that the night vision glasses that would be essential for my mission would not be in this mouldy old brick building. I was right, they weren't!

I threw the rope over my shoulder and put the wirecutters in the side pocket of my black jeans. I closed the door and headed back to the fence. I was in the middle of the gravely surface when I saw the telltale flickering light from the large building that told me someone was welding inside. I knew it was Tommy. Who else would be mad enough to be welding at such a late hour? It seemed crazy even by Tommy's standards. I sneaked over to get a better look.

The only way to see anything would be from one of the few windows that had not been boarded up. The easiest one to access was about ten metres up. Fortunately, Tommy's erratic stacking of old scrap cars meant that several of the burnt out carcasses were leaning against the wall of the building, making a handy, if somewhat, treacherous ladder up to the window.

I balanced on the roof of a 1986 Vauxhall Cavalier before scrambling up to the top of the heap and stretching upwards to grab the sill of the window.

I didn't look in the window straight away. I was pretty sure it was Tommy in there but, if it wasn't, I might just be looking in on some international crime lord. A tough nut who was about to commit a grisly crime and, if they caught any witnesses to their activities, those unlucky enough would never be seen again. Or, if they were ever to be found again, it would be at the bottom of a deep lake somewhere wearing concrete boots.

But, as they say, fortune favours the brave, although I'm not sure any fortune was to be made in this case. I carefully raised my head above the sill. When I could finally look into the building all I could see was the brilliant, blinding welding arc. I immediately looked away, I had avoided welder's eye so far and this wasn't the best time to start.

I waited for the loud buzzing of the welding to stop, took a breath and looked in. Down below there was a cloud of smoke and fumes generated by the heavy welding.

Sure enough, when the welder lifted his mask up, it was Tommy. I guess the international crime lord was doing something else tonight.

Tommy stood back to admire his work, and I tried to see exactly what it was he was making.

It took quite a few moments for the smoke to disappear and, even then, I wasn't quite sure what I was looking at. I had to smile at one point, because from up here it almost looked like the upside down head of a giant metal man. I shook my head; I must have made a mistake so I tilted my head to get a better view.

My mouthed dropped open for, sure enough, there below was the enormous head of a giant metal man. I thought back to what Tommy had made me weld over the past week or so. The two wedge shaped constructions with five buckets welded on the end - giant feet. The lampposts welded together at slight angles – legs. Tommy was making himself some enormous bloke completely out of scrap!

There was only one question that I could think of- why? I looked again in case I had made a mistake – I hadn't.

The nose was made up of a car door, old metal railings for the hair, dustbin lids for the ears, old metal balls for eyes and, the master stroke, a giant chain made into the shape of a mouth.

My brain was racing with all sorts of ideas as to why someone like Tommy would be making a giant metal man. Had he joined some strange cult? Had he been visited by beings from another world, large metal people who he was now worshipping? Or was he just simply well and truly round the twist?

I climbed carefully down the pile and made my way to the fence. As I climbed over I looked back, expecting to see a giant metal man bursting through the roof of the building and heading my way.

It didn't happen so I set off on my main mission of the night, grappling hook and all.

CHAPTER THIRTY-EIGHT

As I climbed over the two-metre high wire fence at the recycling centre I could see the security office lights were on. My heart was thumping but I managed to get close enough to the office to notice that the security guard had his feet up on his desk and was watching TV.

I stood there for a moment until I was confident enough that I was in the clear and moved towards the huge recycling plant. The black shadow cast by the moon, that was set high up in the sky behind the plant, made it much easier to get closer than I had expected. The height of the building cast a long deep shadow, since there were no security lights in this area. I made it all the way to the loading bay, at the far end of the building, and hid behind two wheelie bins.

Surprisingly, there was quite a lot of activity, although most of it seemed to be taking place at the other side of the building. The loading bay was fully illuminated by a bank of security lights and so my black outfit would show up like a beetle on a snowball. I had to find another way to get round to the other side of the building.

It was only when I looked upwards that I noticed a maintenance ladder leading up to a gantry, about thirty metres high, that spanned the roof of the building.

I stayed still for a moment in the dark shadows and, for the first time, thought about what I was about to do. Although I had been keeping my nose clean, if you discount the stuff in the mine, I knew that just by being here I was risking my whole future. But the reason I was sitting in the shadows was for one reason only, Dad. It had finally dawned on me that my Dad was up to his neck in the sticky stuff. I had admitted to myself that he was probably onto a loser trying to take on Spindle Industries and their professional legal team. The only way out for him was for me to try to unearth something dirty about Spindle himself. Mum had always told me that two wrongs didn't make a right but maybe a bigger wrong might just mean that a smaller, well intentioned, wrong might be looked upon more favourably.

I took a big breath and then climbed onto the top of one of the wheelie bins. The first rung of the ladder was too high to reach from the ground so I was going to have to summon up cat-like agility to reach it. The only trouble was I didn't possess any cat-like agility so I had to settle for using the grappling iron to hook onto the bottom rung. As I pushed myself off the wheelie bin I found myself swinging with a couple of metres of fresh air beneath me, more warthog-like than cat-like! I waited until I felt I had summoned enough strength and then hauled my way up onto the rungs. Mr. Benson, my PE teacher, would have been proud of me!

I looked around the compound, fearful that I had made a racket clambering up but there was no one to be seen.

I climbed all the way to the top of the ladder and soon found myself on the gantry, from where I could see the whole compound and beyond. Even though it was dark I could see the silhouette of the hills that surrounded Larkley, the estate with our house somewhere in the middle. I could even make out my school.

The sight of the school made me stop in my tracks. Why was I being so stupid? Did I really think I could save my Dad? Would all this end in disaster?

Before I had chance to change my mind and make a bolt for freedom, the door of the security cabin opened down below and the lanky security officer stepped out. I lowered myself down, as quietly as I could, onto the metal grating of the gantry and peered downwards. The security officer was blissfully unaware of the intruder on his patch and proceeded to lock the cabin door, making his way over to a lorry with an empty trailer. He started to talk to the lorry driver and it seemed they were ready for a good old chinwag.

I had no choice now, I couldn't go back down the ladder so I had to get myself across the roof and down the other side of the building. I made my way across the roof, as silently as possible.

Fortunately there was another ladder waiting for me at the other side and I quickly shimmied down it.

I was about to make a break for the outer fence when something made me look inside an open door of the building. There was no one to be seen and I could see the steps leading down to the base of one of the towers. I could also see that the door was slightly ajar.

I could sense the devil and the angel on each of my shoulders. The angel was telling me to go home. Guess what the devil was suggesting and, guess which one my stupid little brain listened to?

The sprint across the floor and down the steps could not have lasted more than five seconds but it felt like eternity. Before entering the door I hesitated. I was scared of what might be in there. What if Cold Eyes was waiting in there, wearing an apron and revving up his chainsaw? Then I thought of Dad, thought of Harry Spindle, and went in.

As I closed the door behind me I realised that it was completely dark inside. However, the noise was overwhelming; a thunderous, rattling mechanical noise, which seemed like it was coming from all directions. I could feel the panic rising in my gut but tried to control it. I knew that, if I did lose the plot, I would be caught for sure.

I took a few deep breaths and waited until the blood racing through my veins had settled down. I was still near the door; I had hardly moved and I knew that usually there was a good chance there would be a light switch nearby. After several seconds of feeling around on the surface of the cold wall I finally found the square switch and turned it on. The room was bare, apart from a huge, steel casing directly in front of me. The casing led down from the ceiling, forming a dogleg and was supported by a series of metal legs. The huge casing extended the full length of the room and disappeared through the far wall. The ear splitting rattling was coming from inside the casing, as if a million objects were being smashed about inside. The casing was completely sealed but I noticed there was a hatch set halfway along the section towards the wall.

I made my way to the hatch and climbed up to it.

I undid the two steel latches and opened the hatch. Inside the casing I could see a conveyor belt with hundreds of unrecognisable objects slowly passing by. I stood there watching for several moments before it dawned on me what I was looking at - rubbish. The smell was overwhelming and I had to turn my head away for a moment.

It was then that I heard voices outside the door; I turned around to see the door handle turning. I had to make a quick decision.

As I rushed along the conveyor belt, tumbling among a mass of the town's rubbish, it occurred to me that jumping through the hatch might not be the best decision I'd ever made. After about half a second I was wishing I had taken my chances back in the room. I was being battered from side to side, thrown up and down in amongst the stinking, soggy contents of the metal chute.

Then the worst thought of all popped into my head. Where was this conveyor belt heading? Could this be that horrendous Willy Wonka type ending for me? Gobbled up by the jaws of some huge mechanical monstrosity into tiny bits, or would it lead into the towers which would turn me into toast.

I tried to stop myself getting pulled into the black oblivion beyond. There was nothing to grab onto; the walls were incredibly smooth and I guess this was to stop any of the bags of rubbish from snagging and causing a blockage.

I knew I was screaming but the noise that surrounded me was so incredible that even I couldn't hear myself.

Then suddenly I found myself back in the cold night air and tumbling from the chute into a container several metres below. The landing was pretty smooth, although my shoulder hit something solid. I tried to stand but my legs sank in the rubbish and the sides of the metal container were too slimy to get a grip.

I was about to make one superhuman effort to get myself up when I heard a diesel motor starting. Then suddenly a head appeared over the edge of the container, the head of the lorry driver I had seen the security officer talking to earlier. I had obviously fallen into the back of a lorry trailer. He was casting a net over the edge of his open topped trailer to keep the contents in. I pulled a couple of bin bags over my head and sank back into the rubbish. Something was leaking a putrid, foul liquid over my head and I tried to sink deeper into the rubbish to avoid it. I felt the lorry moving and threw the bag off, wiping whatever it was away from my face. I was a bit light headed but tried to ignore it and focus.

I was escaping from the recycling centre in the back of a lorry full of rubbish; rubbish that I guessed Harry Spindle was going to dump somewhere. The big problem was how I was going to get off this lorry, before I too was tipped into some waiting hole in the middle of the night?

CHAPTER THIRTY-NINE

I awoke with a start as the lorry screeched to a halt. Somehow, despite the fact that I had no idea where I was going, or what was going to happen to me, I had fallen asleep in the back of the lorry. Then I remembered the putrid fumes coming from one of the bin bags. The vapours must have knocked me out. Maybe someone had chucked out some dodgy chemicals in their bin bags!

I slowly scrambled to the back of the trailer, managing to stick my head up so I could see through a hole in the netting and finally get some fresh air. Since I didn't know how long I had been asleep, and it was pitch black out there, I had no idea how far away from Larkley I had travelled, and that was quite a disturbing thought. I suddenly felt very lost and alone and wished I had stayed at home.

The lorry had stopped at a set of gates, at the start of a track and I finally realised where I was- at the bottom of the road leading up to the mine!

I could hear voices at the front of the lorry and, after much scrambling along the length of the lorry, I managed to peek over the edge.

The lorry driver was out of his cab and he was talking to someone who had his back to me. When the large man turned around to point something out to the driver I immediately sank into the stinking but now welcoming sea of bin bags – it was Cold Eyes.

I stayed still for a moment and then tilted my head so I could pick up snippets of the conversation.

"Three more tonight," the driver said.

"Good, get zis shifted and back on zee road now," said a heavily accented voice that I knew, without looking, belonged to Cold Eyes.

The door of the lorry was slammed shut and it began to make its way slowly up the track, seeming to hit every pothole on the way. Fortunately the bags of rubbish made pretty good padding. I managed to stand up and peer over the edge to see the gate to the fluorspar mine passing by; we were going further up the track, which led to the old mine that Sparky had mentioned. I noticed the lights of a 4 x 4 following behind us on the track. Great! Cold Eyes was following us. I ducked out of sight.

Now I was in even more danger. I knew I had to make the right decision, otherwise I wouldn't be leaving these dark hills tonight- or possibly ever.

I kept my head low as the lorry finally reached the top of the winding track and started to drop down the other side. From what I could make out we were dropping into some sort of huge crater- a quarry perhaps. In the far distance I could see the spotlights of another vehicle, which appeared to be moving slowly back and forth. As we drew closer I could see it was a bulldozer. In the spotlights I could see an entrance to another mineshaft. From my vantage point in the back of the lorry it looked like the bulldozer was pushing a sea of rubbish bags towards the mine entrance and down it, like a huge rubbish chute.

When the lorry came to an eventual stop the lorry driver hopped out and walked over to the bulldozer.

"Now then Dave. Reckon it's gonna be a long night again."

The door of the dozer slid open. "Aye, and the Ukrainian devil just makes it that bit longer. He's in an even worse mood than usual."

The "Ukrainian Devil" was obviously Cold Eyes.

They continued to talk while I took a few moments to finally work everything out. Although the details were still a bit hazy I now knew that Harry Spindle was on the fiddle on a huge scale. Whatever those two, big towers were supposed to do they weren't doing it. Instead of reducing the town's rubbish into some sort of compost, and the rest being recycled, the rubbish was actually going out of the bottom of the towers, through the steel chutes and into the back of waiting lorries. Then the rubbish was taken to this quarry and buried in the middle of the night down the mineshaft. It was like sweeping the rubbish under the carpet, but on a gigantic scale.

"Stop zee talking and vork."

I guessed the Ukrainian devil had turned up. I knew that at any second the lorry driver, or worse, Cold Eyes himself, would appear as the netting was removed. My only advantage was the element of surprise but there was no way that I could make a break for it. The jump from the trailer would be too high and I couldn't see the ground below. I would just have to wait until the trailer began to tip upwards and hope I could scramble downwards and away into the darkness.

I ducked back into the sea of black plastic bags, while the net was removed and the hydraulics kicked in to start tipping the trailer. I waited until the trailer was at an angle that allowed the bin bags to start sliding out and then made my move. As I slid through the open tailgate of the lorry I let go and hit the floor running.

I would have bolted off into the blackness of the night but I ran straight into, what felt like, a solid brick wall. It was only when I realised that the solid brick wall had grabbed me around the neck with an arm of steel that I looked up. Even in the darkness I could make out the icy, blue stare of Cold Eyes.

CHAPTER FORTY

"Time to talk little man."

I looked up to see Cold Eyes standing in front of me. He was barely visible in the shadows of the darkened room into which he had dragged me. Suddenly a brilliant light was turned on and I shielded my eyes from the glare.

I could make out another figure standing behind the blinding light.

I tried to be brave. "Er, I reckon you should be letting me go now."

Cold Eyes chuckled coldly. "Yeah, sure and ve vill give you some cash too, ha."

I guess he was joking on both counts.

"No, really I think it's probably best for us all if you let me go."

"I guess it vas you at zee recycling centre earlier tonight?"

I had to play dumb; to admit anything would be a big mistake at this stage. "Recycling centre?"

"Yah, zee same recycling centre you sneaked into tonight – ve have zee cameras everywhere little man."

I watched as he walked away and stood behind the light talking to the other person. From what I could see, and hear, it appeared that they were arguing.

I looked around for some sort of escape but there wasn't anything obvious. I was in a concrete room with a few millimetres of water on the floor. I was shivering from the cold and damp. There was nothing else in the room apart from the three of us, the chair, on which I found myself sitting and the giant tripod holding the light up.

As Cold Eyes started to walk back a real sense of panic began to set in the pit of my stomach. Where was I? Would I get out of here? Would I die looking like a Goth?

I tried to crane my neck to peer around the light and managed to catch a glimpse of the other person who was now smoking a cigar. Harry Spindle smoked cigars. Of course, who else did I think it was going to be?

I had to try and blag my way out. "You do anything to me and you're going down, down forever Mayor Spindle."

Harry remained silent but Cold Eyes held his stomach with laughter. "I have been in and out of zee vorst prisons most of my life so don't threaten me."

He pulled out a rope from behind the light and started to walk towards me. I tried to move out of the way but, for a big bloke, he moved quickly.

He pushed me back down and tied me tightly to the chair; the knots wouldn't move a millimetre. Maybe, he had been a member of his local scout group back in the Ukraine; I doubted it somehow!

As Cold Eyes walked away I tried once more to see the other person but the light was suddenly turned off and, for a moment, the bright white shadow, that the light had left behind. blinded me. When I opened my eyes it was pure darkness and very quiet; I was alone.

I sat there in the dark, alone, tied to the chair, hoping that Mum and Dad had not yet discovered that the lump in my bed was actually my punch-bag and not me!

Suddenly the door opened a few millimetres, someone stepped in and the light exploded back into life. I had to close my eyes for several moments.

I blinked slowly until my eyes were fully open but whoever had walked into the room stayed behind the light.

"Okay, what do you want from me?"

There was no answer.

"Yeah, yeah you've scared me enough now."

Still no reply.

"Please." To be honest I was close to crying.

"Nelson Burns for once can't you shut your big, stupid gob."

My eyes were suddenly wide open as I heard my name but, as the owner of the voice stepped into the light, I nearly fell backwards, chair and all.

"Douglas Spindle - what the heck do you want?"

Doug the Slug stood in front of the light, so I couldn't see his face. Therefore I wasn't sure if he was laughing. I guessed he probably was.

"You must be enjoying this?"

Douglas looked around towards the door. "Is that what you think Burns?"

"Probably. Hardly bosom buddies are we?"

"No. You're right but, at the same time, I don't want this to happen to you, not in my family's name. As soon as I saw you being carted in by Dad and his main man I knew I'd have to help you."

He stepped behind me and started to untie the ropes.

"What are you doing?" I asked suspiciously.

Douglas kept untying the knots. "For once in your life Burns, shut it."

Suddenly my hands were free and I stood up. I attempted a defensive stance but cramp in both my legs got the better of me.

Douglas looked at me with a resigned expression on his face. "So you think I've untied you so that we can have a scrap, do you Burns?"

"I don't know, did you?"

Douglas shook his head. "I'm here to get you out of this place and stop my Dad doing something stupid."

I was gobsmacked. Here was my arch-enemy about to help me escape.

"You ready?"

"I guess so."

Douglas headed towards the door and turned off the light. He opened the door and peeked outside – he waited for a few moments before waving me over. I hesitated. Was this a trap? I had to take the chance that Douglas was telling the truth.

"Right, when you get to the track start running and don't stop until you get home," he whispered.

He stepped out of the door and I followed. We were in the quarry and I could see the lights of Larkley twinkling in the dark of the valley below. I looked behind to see that I had been kept in an old, steel container.

Douglas grabbed me by the arm and led me through the dark, until we were on a gravely track.

He stopped and turned round. "Just keep on this track and it will lead down to the main road."

He turned and was about to walk away.

"Douglas," I whispered.

"What?" He said impatiently.

"Thanks."

Douglas was silent for a moment. "I did this for my Dad, not you. Now get the hell out of here."

I started to run into the darkness, stumbling down the track but managing to stay upright.

CHAPTER FORTY-ONE

By the time I reached the back door of our house birds were singing the dawn chorus which, I had to admit, was not a sound I had heard that often. A horizon of mist was hovering above our front lawn.

As I crept along our garden path carrying my bike that I had collected from where I had stashed it near the recycling centre, every step sounded like I was crushing a thousand eggshells. I parked my bike up and opened the back door.

I made my way through the kitchen past the mighty Kickstart, who appeared to be chasing some imaginary rabbit in his dreams, and crept upstairs. I closed my bedroom door and moved the punch-bag off my bed. There were some computer print outs spread out over my duvet. I picked them up and noticed they were geological maps of the area around Larkley, in particular the area near Water Mill Cottages. Freddy, amazingly, had taken the time to highlight that the source of the stream at Water Mill Cottages ran down from the hills. Exactly the same place in the old quarry where Spindle and his gang were dumping rubbish. Was that the reason that Miss Steint, Old Jed and Tommy Ratson had gone bonkers? I hoped that Mum's friends would prove it was so with the results of the water tests.

I was exhausted but as I looked at the clock I realised it was only 4:47 AM.

Did I tell Mum and Dad that I had been out and broken every rule I had promised to obey? Or did I tell them about Cold Eyes and about Harry Spindle's huge con? I closed my eyes to think about these tricky problems.

These heavy questions were still on my mind the next time I opened my eyes. I rolled over and expected the clock to say maybe 4:49 or something similar – certainly not 9:55!

For the first time I could remember I had slept in, and on the worst possible day to do it. The night's events must have been more exhausting than I realised but how come my Mum hadn't woken me up, as she had done without fail since I had started school?

At least there was no need for me to get dressed; I was still decked out in my black gear, although I was aware of how much I must stink.

I knocked on my Mum and Dad's bedroom door, even though it was ajar and the amount of daylight shining through told me the curtains had been opened. I hesitated but there was no response to my tentative knock, I was reluctant to enter but knew I had to. I summoned the courage and looked in- it was empty.

I galloped down the stairs to find a note waiting for both Freddy and me on the kitchen table.

"Boys, your Dad and I have had to leave early to get to court in plenty of time. Leave the place tidy and lock the door behind you. And Nelson, make sure you get to the referral unit and then the yard in time, do your work and come straight home."

I felt knowing eyes boring into me and looked down at Kickstart. "Well old son, this is the mother of all pickles. What should I do? Give me a sign."

Kickstart looked at me for a second before starting to chew at his back leg, making a sterling effort to get rid of a tick that was bothering him.

I don't know why he's looking at me with that strange expression on his face. All I'm trying to do is stop this pesky flea from biting my bits. He is lucky he never seems to have the kind of itches us dogs do, although he seems to like scratching his back end a lot!

That was the sign: get rid of an old itch! I picked up my keys and headed to the door. "Kickstart you genius, every dog has his day in court old son."

CHAPTER FORTY-TWO

The old, but magnificent, magistrates' courts were to be found in the high street and as I walked up the stone steps I could sense lots of eyes were watching me.

"Nelson my man, thanks for the backing dude."

I noticed that Mad Mikey had neither covered his yellow Mohawk, nor his flaming spear tattoo for his court appearance, although he had made the effort to wear a three piece suit, albeit a tartan one! He might have been as mad as a frothing dingo but he had style – or sorts!

"What time you up?"

Mad Mikey pulled an antique looking pocket-watch from his waistcoat pocket. In a strange way he made a striking figure.

"About 12 seconds my man. Give me a handshake for luck."

Mad Mikey held out his hand and grabbed mine like he was intending to squeeze the bones out.

"They don't scare me and I like the challenge – bring it on," he declared.

A rather short, prim and proper looking man, the court usher, stepped out from one of the huge doors, which I guessed led the way to the magistrates court.

"Michael Cornelius Given."

Mad Mikey looked at me and winked. "Bet ya would never have guessed that for my middle name eh!" He slapped me on the back and turned to the court usher.

"That'll be me gov. Ready to rock 'n roll."

The usher looked up at him and tried to speak but only succeeded in getting his bottom lip to quiver viciously. He opened the door and beckoned for Mad Mikey to walk in.

As the usher followed him, still in an apparent state of shock and closed the door I could hear a gasp from within the courtroom.

"Nelson – what are you doing here?"

I turned to see my very worried looking Mum steaming towards me.

"You should be at work. This is no place for you."

"Tommy doesn't need me today," I lied.

Mum held her nose. "And what is that awful smell?"

I looked behind me innocently, realising that a night spent rolling around in rubbish would have left me smelling like a tramp's vest.

"Well your Dad is next and you can't come in."

I could see Dad sitting in a side room. He was talking to someone.

"But…"

"There are no buts for this one Nelson." Just the sound of her angry voice was enough to tell me that my life would be ended in an instant if I disobeyed her.

"There's something I need to tell you."

"I'm sure you have love, but it'll have to wait."

"It can't, this will help Dad – honestly."

Mum smiled and stroked my hair. "I know you care, so much it hurts Nelson, despite often being a prize prat, but the truth is there is nothing you can do now."

"What you doing here son?" Dad said, as he approached, holding a whole pile of files and papers. I have to say he looked pretty impressive in his dark suit, less in your face than Mad Mikey but that was probably a good thing.

"Dad I've seen something- last night."

Mum looked at Dad in dismay. "Still having nightmares son?"

"No, no, you don't understand- I wasn't asleep last night, I wasn't even in my bed."

Mum's eyes narrowed. "Nelson, I don't have time to listen to your stupid stories."

"You weren't up at Water Mill Cottages again by any chance son?" Dad asked.

"Water Mill Cottages?" I offered innocently.

"Miss Steint tells me you paid her a visit." Dad gestured to the side room and, as I looked, my pupil referral officer turned round to smile at me. I couldn't help but stare at her wig!

"Miss Steint's here today with one of her pupils and told me she bumped into you the other day."

I was about to try and pull my head out of the man trap I felt I was heading for, when suddenly the doors of the court flew open and the tartan blur that was Mad Mikey appeared.

"Ha, fifty quid and bound over to keep the peace for a year – I could do that blindfolded," he beamed victoriously.

The prim and proper usher stepped out. "William Steven Burns."

"Right here we go," Dad said, as he stepped into the court.

Mum turned to me. "Nelson, you'd better be at home when I get back otherwise you're grounded for infinity and beyond."

Mum walked into the court and the usher closed the door.

Everything was a mess and it seemed I was powerless to do anything about it. Then I saw Eloise standing outside the court doors crying, and I guessed the mess was about to get much bigger.

CHAPTER FORTY-THREE

"What do you mean he's gone back to the mine?" I whispered, as we stood outside the courthouse.

Eloise looked at the floor. "He said something about finding the mother of all gems. What is he talking about Nelson and what mine does he mean?"

"He is a prize bozo, I told him not to go back, not after..." I immediately stopped myself.

"After what?" Eloise said, with an immediate look of suspicion. "What have you two been up to?"

I thought about lying but dismissed the idea immediately. So I told her the whole story. Everything. Nothing was spared.

"You absolute pair of idiots," she screamed at me. "He could be lying up there dead right now."

It was my turn to look at the ground. "I told him not to go back there – honest."

Eloise closed her eyes. "You know he'll have gone back there to get this stupid rock to impress you."

I looked back up into her accusing eyes. "Well let's go and get him."

"Yes, lets," she sighed.

"First there's something I need to do."

I saw Jenny Regatta standing near the front of the courts, she was looking upwards and TJ was pointing his camera up to the roof of the court building.

As I walked over to her I followed the angle of TJ's camera to see what was so interesting up on the roof.

"Looks like our prickly friend is back in business." I said, as the giant hedgehog, chained around the court's chimney pot, waved his "Justice for Larkley's nature lovers" banner aloft. Mad Mikey really was a determined nutcase, I'd give him that.

As Jenny Regatta looked back up I could have sworn she almost looked impressed.

"Can I have a quick word Jenny? It's real important."

"Sorry son, we're in the middle of a news item here."

"I have another story that could be the biggest you've ever covered."

This caught her attention. "You've got five seconds."

I looked around, making sure we were not being overheard. "I know what Harry Spindle is really doing with this town's rubbish."

Jenny's eyes widened. "How?"

"Let's just say I know first hand."

Jenny looked really interested now. "Prove it."

"Meet me here in an hour and you could be picking up the Pulitzer Prize next year." I scribbled directions to the old quarry on a piece of paper, handed it to her and headed off to my next target.

PC Ben Riley, once again, seemed to be on nothing more than crowd control.

"He's in trouble now Nelson."

I watched as Mad Mikey gave a bow to the crowd that had started to gather in front of the courts.

"Somehow I don't think he's too bothered."

"He is committed to the cause, I'll give him that."

"The press seem to like him." PC Riley said, as Jenny continued to look up at Mad Mikey, with a slight smile on her normally hard face.

"I've gotta go somewhere PC Riley. Right now! And if you meet me there in an hour you might just get that big case you've always wanted."

I scribbled the directions to the quarry down once more and handed them to PC Riley. I had asked for the hour head start because I hoped that when I got there I could find Sparky and stop him getting into trouble but if I couldn't I would need PC Riley's help.

"If this calms down I'll see what I can do. No promises though Nelson."

I started to walk towards Eloise.

"Nelson?"

I turned around.

"This isn't one of your wind ups is it?"

"For once you've really gotta believe me PC Riley."

CHAPTER FORTY-FOUR

I felt really nervous as we approached the road up to the mine.

"How long have you two clowns been coming here?" Eloise asked. She was sitting on the crossbar of my bike as I peddled for my life, or maybe Sparky's life!

"Not long," I said vaguely.

"You know what I think?" said Eloise. "The prize goon award goes to you Nelson Burns. My brother is an idiot but at least he is an idiot who isn't under the microscope, with the possibility of ending up in the gutter if he gets caught."

"Let's concentrate our efforts on finding Sparky." I urged.

Eloise shook her head in dismay.

"Ah, here's the track up the quarry", I said, seeing the locked gates.

Eloise jumped down from the crossbar and I hid the bike behind a wall. Picking up a large rock I proceeded to smash it down on the lock.

"What are you doing Nelson?" Eloise shouted.

"We need this gate open to let the cavalry in – if PC Riley and Jenny Regatta turn up I don't want any excuse for them turning away."

Eventually the lock broke away and we headed up the track. We ran up through the trees alongside the track for cover. This time no trucks or Ukrainian devils in 4 x 4's passed by.

When we reached the crossroads I could still see the fresh tyre marks, from the previous night, heading up to the quarry on the other side of the hill and pointed them out to Eloise. I gestured towards the skinny track that led to the fluorspar mine.

Suddenly there was an almighty boom and everything seemed to shake.

Eloise grabbed my shoulder. "What was that?"

"Either an earthquake, or someone's just set off an explosion."

We both looked at one another, thinking the same thought.

"Sparky!"

We started to run towards the mine.

Sure enough, when we got to the mine entrance, there was Sparky's pushbike parked up. A plume of dust bellowed from the mouth of the mine.

"Sparky," I shouted several times but there was no response.

"You okay to go in there?" I asked, as we looked up at the three sets of rickety steps that led to the mine entrance.

"See you at the top," Eloise said. I had trouble keeping up and she reached the entrance to the mine several seconds before me.

"It's pretty dark and wet in there?" I said, hoping to put some fear into, what was turning out to be, a fairly fearless heart.

"Nothing's gonna stop me getting hold of that dingbat."

"Here put one of these on." I said, as I threw her one of the strap-on bicycle lights that she herself had given us. Once we had put on our hard helmets and slipped the lights on I tied a rope around my waist. I wasn't taking any chances and tied the other end around Eloise's waist.

We headed into the mine and soon found ourselves turning on the lights on our helmets, as we stepped into the blanket of darkness within.

We quickly edged our way around the rock pool and soon came up against the wall of rock, under which I knew Sparky's "Mother of All Gems" was waiting.

The cave was suddenly filled with a huge, crashing boom, followed by a billowing cloud of dust that came through the gap under the rock.

"Cover up quick," I said to Eloise, as we both pulled our t-shirts up and over our mouths and noses. The makeshift facemasks only kept a fraction of the dust out and soon we were both coughing harshly. It was pointless trying to move until we could see where we were going.

"Damn it Sparky, you are such a pain." I said as I lay flat on the floor and started to squeeze through the gap. The length of the rope meant that Eloise had to stay close behind. Although the dust was clearing it still made the squeeze through that little bit more difficult.

When we got through to the other side we stood up and wafted away the dust.

When it finally cleared, there in front of us, sitting on a pile of fallen rocks was Sparky, still in one piece holding what I guessed was the "Mother of all Gems", a huge green and purple block of fluorspar.

"Isn't she a beauty – we're gonna be rich."

I looked at him in bewilderment.

"Don't tell me you've just blasted that rock out?"

Sparky waved a hand dismissively. "Relax Rabies. Just a wee speck of black powder I borrowed from of one of Uncle Tommy's old mates."

Eloise stormed up to her brother. "You idiot, you absolute idiot. Don't you realise you could have brought this whole place down and squashed us all, not just your own selfish backside!"

"In my defence I didn't know you two were in here."

Eloise got hold of Sparky's collar and yanked his face towards hers. "That's not the point boghead. You know some of us care about you, even if you don't".

Sparky pointed to the back of the cavern. "I hid behind that big rock; I'm telling you there was nothing to it. Hardly anything moved – piece of cake this blasting lark."

As he said this a stream of dust started to fall onto Sparky's hardhat. He looked up as the dust began to turn into a steady stream of small rocks, followed by, what I can only describe as, an earth tremor.

"Piece of cake eh!" I said, grabbing him by the arm and pulling him towards me, just as a huge rock fell down from the cavern's ceiling. He looked at me in terror, as more rocks started to tumble down and the three of us scrambled to the back of the cave and behind the big rock. We huddled together, arms over heads, with Eloise squashed beneath us, as the whole cave rocked and huge boulders crashed down. It seemed to last an eternity. I could feel some smaller rocks bouncing off our hard hats.

Eventually the rocks stopped raining down and we were able to check ourselves for damage. Eloise stood up to look down towards the rock face.

"We got lucky there," I declared.

"I think our luck just ran out." Eloise whispered.

Sparky and I stood and followed the direction of Eloise's gaze. Sure enough, the gap at the bottom of the rock face, our one and only exit from this rock solid chamber, was blocked.

CHAPTER FORTY-FIVE

"It's no good. It's not budging an inch." I gasped, as Sparky and I tried to use an old wooden beam to move one of the bigger rocks away from the face.

Eloise launched herself on top of Sparky. After a couple of seconds she stopped hitting him and collapsed on top of him, tears finally taking over.

"What are we going to do? We're trapped and for what- a stupid bit of rock?" Eloise sobbed.

I looked at the massive boulders that blocked our way to freedom. I knew that we were in serious trouble and that no one knew where we were.

"We're going to die in here aren't we?" Eloise sobbed again.

I tried to answer but I couldn't.

"You youngsters ain't gonna die, at least not today."

The gruff voice echoed around the cave and the three of us stood bolt upright in an instant, like a family of startled meerkats.

Then I saw the face, the same wizened old face I thought I had seen near the rock pool on the other side of the wall the first time I had entered the mine. When I blinked the wizened old face started to rise upwards, mainly because it was attached to the body of a wizened old man!

Eloise grabbed Sparky, Sparky grabbed me and I grabbed them both to form a collective ring that would hopefully protect us from the ghost of a wizened old man.

The spectre moved closer, sliding over rocks slowly, like a python heading towards its petrified prey. He was really old, older than anyone I had ever seen, although there wasn't an ounce of fat on his muscled body. His face was blackened with dust and his clothes were falling off his back.

He moved slowly and silently up to the three of us, before suddenly bursting into a completely toothless smile.

"Hello Nelson, the name's Chester McWinney, I think I know ya old man son."

The name sounded familiar but my brain was frazzled. Survival was my only thought.

"Good man Billy Burns, one of the best."

I suddenly realised that this wasn't some sort of ghostly vision but a very real wizened, old man and I now knew who he was – the old miner who had rescued the Council's plant pots and whom Dad had tried to save.

"Er, where've you come from?" I asked nervously.

"Been down here since those plonkers in Larkley had me nicked. Mind you the company's better down here."

Dad's stories about this bloke had made him a folk hero in our house and I wasn't about to be spooked by him. I couldn't say the same for Eloise and Sparky, who looked scared stiff.

"So you fluorspar prospectors have got yourselves in one serious pickle ain't ya?" Chester McWinney looked down at Eloise. "And got this little lady in the same mess, with no way out. A pretty stupid pair of lads you got yourself here sweetheart."

Sparky looked at me and I looked down at the floor. That was it then. If this old goat, who had spent the past ten years living in these old tunnels, didn't know a way out, we were well and truly scuppered.

"Unless we take the other way out of course." The old toothless miner said casually.

And before we knew it Chester McWinney had already set off and reached the top of the cavern, without us even noticing he had moved.

"Well come on, unless you fancy spending the next ten years or so with me for company." By the time we reached the top of the cave he had disappeared.

"Here, this way," Eloise said, as she discovered a well hidden passage, with a flickering light casting shadows some way down below. Eloise vanished down it in an instant and both Sparky and I quickly followed her.

The tunnels were freezing and we tried to keep the cold at bay by moving swiftly. The skinny tunnels looked like they had been access routes to the deeper parts of the mine. They were propped up every two or three metres, by wooden props, with joists across the top. The floor was pretty smooth, as if a lot of traffic and pit boots had passed this way a long time ago. There was no sign of Chester McWinney but we could hear his mad cackle echoing along the walls.

Suddenly the roof opened up into a cavern and the old miner was waiting for us. He hadn't even broken sweat. As Eloise, Sparky and I bent over trying to catch our breath, I noticed that this area was much warmer.

But then I noticed the smell! An overwhelming and stifling rancid odour that hung in the air and made the three of us gag.

"What is that stink?" I said, putting a hand to my mouth.

Chester McWinney rubbed his head. "Oh, that'll be the rubbish."

I looked at Sparky and Eloise knowingly. "The rubbish?"

"Yeah, the stuff that some clowns up on top have been bulldozing down one of the deeper shafts for months now. There's gotta be thousands and thousand of tonnes of it down here."

"Why didn't you tell someone?" I said in bewilderment.

"Most people think I'm dead so who'd believe me?"

"But it could help my Dad."

His ears seem to prick up. "Help your Dad; is he in trouble?"

"Yeah, and he needs all the help he can get."

"Anything I can do lad?" He obviously hadn't forgotten my Dad from all those years ago.

"Getting us out of here and telling everyone what's been going on would be a great start."

I hadn't even finished the sentence and the old timer was off like a young racehorse.

"Better keep up then kids," he shouted over his shoulder.

We carried on for several more minutes until I noticed that running was becoming more and more difficult and it dawned on me that we were starting to move upwards.

We soon found ourselves in another open area with two tunnels leading off. However, Chester McWinney looked alarmed and was sniffing the air.

"You smell that?" Chester McWinney said, looking concerned. "Something's burning."

The three of us found ourselves acting like sniffer dogs at an airport.

"I find the occasional bag smouldering but this is different." Chester McWinney walked over to one of the tunnels. "Right, you three take this one and it will lead you to the outside. It comes out in thick bushes just above the quarry."

"And you?" Eloise asked.

"This other tunnel leads to a second shaft; this is my home and I need to put that fire out."

I knew he wasn't intending to come with us and I could understand; he had not been in the outside world for a long time.

I shook his hand. "I'll tell my Dad you're alive and well."

"And you tell him thanks Nelson."

Sparky and Eloise shook his hand and then he was gone, running down the other tunnel. We watched the light from his helmet, as it bounced off the tunnel walls, before it eventually faded into the distance.

"Right, let's get up to the light and some fresh air." I suggested. "Now that sounds like a good idea." Eloise agreed.

The incline became steeper and steeper, until we found ourselves climbing hand over foot. Finally we could see what appeared to be a crack of light coming through the rockface.

I could make out trees and bushes through the gap. Without a word Sparky squeezed through the welcome space and into the trees on the outside.

Eloise grabbed me by the arm and dragged me after her brother.

CHAPTER FORTY-SIX

It only took a couple of minutes to fight our way through the trees but we were exhausted by the time we reached a clearing at the edge of a cliff. I looked over at Eloise and Sparky, who were both flaked out on the ground. Within a few seconds the three of us were laughing; laughing with sheer joy because we were alive.

"I'm not sure what you lot are giggling about but enjoy it while you can."

The unmistakable sound of my Mum's voice came from somewhere over the cliff. I peered over the edge to see her standing amongst a small crowd, in the quarry below.

"If you would be so kind as to join us," Mum commanded.

The three of us automatically jumped to our feet and started to scramble down the slope of the quarry face. Waiting down there were Mum, Dad, PC Ben Riley, Jenny Regatta, TJ, Harry Spindle and, oh-my-god, Cold Eyes!

I wanted to tell everyone about what we'd found but I had to pick my moment. Besides, I doubted that Cold Eyes would do anything stupid, at least for now.

"So where've you been son?" Dad asked calmly.

"Oh, we got lost, er, in the old mines."

PC Riley stepped up. "Why did you ask to meet me up here Nelson in this old quarry?"

"Look around young man there's nothing to see." Harry Spindle said, waving his arms about.

I had to control my anger. "That's because it's all been shoved down the mine. You've basically taken all of Larkley's rubbish and stuck it down in the dark below."

Harry purred like the big, fat, smug cat he was. "Mr and Mrs Burns I really do think that you should control your son's obviously fiery temper – before it gets him into trouble."

Dad stepped up to Harry, who clearly recoiled. "He gets that from his Dad unfortunately."

PC Riley pushed his way in between. "Steady Billy. You got off with the charges this morning; so don't rack up any new ones."

"You got off?" I beamed.

Dad's face remained emotionless. "Yep. The magistrates said there was no real evidence, or case history, to make the charges stick."

"A travesty of justice if you ask me," Harry said rather bravely, aware that he had PC Riley as a safety buffer between Dad and himself.

Harry turned to Mum. "As you can see there's nothing to see, so shall we all go home?"

I had to admit Cold Eyes and his crew had done a fantastic job of getting rid of any evidence to suggest that tonnes of waste had been on this site only last night.

They must have shoved it down the throat of the mineshaft, which was now covered in rock. The huge shock that Eloise and I had felt on the track must have been an explosion to seal the mouth of the mine and not Sparky's black powder popping the rock below the surface. And now several massive rocks covered up the evidence of Harry's dirty work.

"I can take you down the old shafts and show you." I offered

"Oh dear Nelson, we can't go down those old tunnels – the health and safety etc." Harry said, with insincere concern.

"Besides, there's probably some pretty explosive gases hanging around down there," said PC Riley.

I turned to Jenny Regatta. "Is there nothing you can do?"

Even Jenny looked downcast. "Not really, without any evidence………"

I was devastated. Surely this wasn't the end – I turned to my Dad and saw him looking back to the cliff face. His face was a mixture of puzzlement and delight. What had he seen?

I turned to see a bedraggled figure running towards us.

"That looks like…" Dad said, without finishing his sentence.

"Chester McWinney," I finished for him.

The figure was waving his arms wildly at us.

Chester seemed different somehow. He now looked like some kind of wild haired, even wilder eyed lunatic.

"How do you know him Nelson?" Dad asked.

"It's a long story."

"He's shouting something," Eloise interrupted.

Chester McWinney was definitely shouting something but it was impossible to tell what.

"I think he's saying something about lying in the pool?" Harry said.

"No, he's saying something about buying some coal," Sparky suggested.

"Wire in the goal?" Dad offered.

It was only then that we all realised exactly what Chester McWinney was saying and why he was waving his arms frantically at us.

"Fire in the hole. Fire in the hole. It's gonna blow."

He didn't have to say another word. We moved as one, turning and running away from the old mine, although TJ was attempting a backward sprint with his camera held aloft in the direction of Chester McWinney.

Harry Spindle and Cold Eyes, however, didn't budge an inch. It seemed as if they were standing their ground, maybe to try and prove their innocence, but eventually Harry's nerve broke and he started running.

When we reached the far edge of the quarry I turned, just in time, to see the first signs of smoke coming from the mine. A low, deep rumbling, which could be felt beneath my feet, followed the smoke. The rumble started to grow, until the ground was actually shaking. And then the top of the hill, under which the mine was located, blew off in what looked like a thousand pieces. The fragments started to rain down on the quarry floor and began reaching our hiding place.

Cold Eyes was still standing in the middle of the quarry, refusing to move as huge projectiles, some of which must have weighed tonnes, whistled past his ears. And then a second explosion followed, as we all huddled together, hoping that we were going to live through what seemed like the end of the world.

This time the clumps that rained down were bits of rubbish, the rubbish that had been buried and sealed in the mine. The fire that had worried Chester McWinney had caused an enormous underground detonation. And now the hill was spewing thousand of tonnes of household waste, like a giant volcano stuffed with the contents of Larkley's dustbins, rather than lava.

Everyone else watched the sky but I looked over at Cold Eyes. He was standing firm under the heavy barrage of a thousand missiles made from rubbish. Finally something felled him, something I recognised.

I was not sure if it was the bright red colour, or the "On Tour" sticker on the windshield but I saw it, even if Cold Eyes didn't. As the remaining section of the motorised mobility scooter smashed him off his feet I ducked back down into the safety of my own little group and waited for the blizzard of household waste to pass.

EPILOGUE

It turned out that the explosion had been caused by a combination of landfill gas and a fire started by a smouldering bag of rubbish. Maybe it was those toxic chemicals I had encountered in the back of the wagon. Weeks later when the police, fire brigade and all sorts of uniformed types had left the town, normality began to return to Larkley.

Mind you I'm not sure if "normality" ever really returned to Larkley.

Although there was no one acting completely out of their trees, you always got the feeling that if you scratched the surface in this place you would stir up a cauldron of lunacy. Mum's friends at the university discovered the presence of various chemicals in the sample I had taken from the stream that flowed alongside Water Mill Cottages; the stream from which the residents had been drinking. Freddy's hydrological maps showed that the stream flowed directly from deep within the mine. It turned out that the rubbish that had been dumped down the mine had created something called "leachate", containing heavy metals such as zinc, which, apparently has been identified as causing short-term psychological problems. In a nutshell, the water from the mines had contaminated the stream; the residents, and even Zombie had drunk the water and they had all gone ape-crazy bonkers.

Old Jed simply returned to sitting on the steps of his allotment, watching the world go by. He seemed happy to be back to his old ways and keep out of the way of his wife. He didn't plant any other electrical appliances!

It turned out that Miss Steint had lost her eyebrows and hair, not because she was ill, but because she believed that she was turning into an albino mole! With a bit of help from various doctors she soon returned to work; her hair (and mono-brow) grew back and she was content to put in a lot of voluntary hours with Mum's environmental group, who took up the plight of the local moles.

Tommy Ratson fared pretty well out of the whole mess. His giant scrap man almost rivalled the Angel of the North as a tourist attraction and he raked it in as people flocked to see it. People came from miles around to see the giant made out of cars, old lampposts, shopping trolleys and metal buckets. I still think the legs and feet were the best parts!

Pc Ben Riley was promoted following the investigation. The fact that he was present when the explosion happened suggested to his bosses that maybe this chubby, cheerful chap was worth more than crowd control.

Jenny Regatta was quickly snapped up by one of the national channels following her exposure of the great Spindle Swindle and TJ became a much sought-after cameraman. It wasn't long after the incident that Jenny Regatta married, and married someone totally unexpected!

A certain news reporter finally tamed Mad Mikey. Yep, that's right, the most unlikely pairing in history, but he and Jenny actually got hitched. Even crazier is that they are expecting a little "scoop" of their own – they are gonna have a baby! Mad Mikey even shaved his yellow Mohawk off and removed the burning spear tattoo from his neck, as a token of his commitment to being a househusband, while Jenny pursued her highflying TV career.

Freddy never did clean his flipping bedroom but he did eventually get a job designing computer games for a hotshot company in London. We visited his flat recently and I was convinced he had taken whatever had died in his bedroom back at home with him!

Eloise has decided she wants to have a career in politics, having been inspired by my Mum. She still sees a lot of my Mum these days, mainly because I see a lot more of Eloise these days.

Mum has also gone back to university, to study marine biology, which I'm really chuffed about. She still manages to run the environmental group as well as looking after Dad and me.

Following the court case, Dad packed in his job as a bin man, his heart was no longer in it and he concentrated his time and energy on starting his own composting company. Although it is not the biggest, or the most profitable recycling company in the country, the one thing it guarantees is that its product is one hundred percent clean and organic.

Chester McWinney disappeared again. I would often ride my bike in the hills overlooking Larkley, but I never did find a clue to his whereabouts. Mind you, I often wondered where Dad used to take that bag of food and drink every Thursday night.

Douglas Spindle was totally changed by the events that exposed his Dad as public enemy number one. His bullying stopped overnight and he concentrated his attentions on becoming one of the nicest kids in town. He even joined Mum's environmental group and the last time I saw him he was happily making feeders for red squirrels.

Harry Spindle was sacked as Mayor, lost all his assets, appeared in court and was heavily fined for all the damage to the environment that he and his cronies had caused. He also got five years in jail for various tax fiddles.

Igor Stravinsky, that's "Cold Eyes" to you and me, amazingly, wasn't killed by the flying half of a bright red motorised scooter. He was badly injured though and was put under constant guard while he recovered in hospital. Eventually he was extradited back to the Ukraine, where he was arrested for an assortment of crimes including fraud, theft, assault and, strangely enough, several counts of illegal fly tipping!

Sparky had somehow managed to put the lump of fluorspar, that had nearly got us all killed, into his backpack and had kept it with him throughout our perilous journey through tunnels and explosions. He found someone who could clean and polish it for him and he sold it to an American collector for a lot of money. Enough money, in fact, to set up his own internet environment company selling everything from water testing kits to composting bins.

Kickstart is still chewing his back leg in the hope of finally getting whatever little fiend is making him itch. He spends a lot of his time down at the yard with his new best friend, Zombie.

As for Zombie he became a mini–celebrity and last time I saw him, was on a news bulletin with the newscaster introducing the world to Zombie's break-dancing skills! He called it "bark-dancing". Some things never change!

As for me, well if you really want to know, my Dad did me proud and won my appeal. Even better, I only had to return to Rockcliffe Comprehensive to finish off my exams, which I blagged as best I could. I won't be going on to college; I've come to the conclusion that the education system and I should part on the best terms possible. I don't want to push my luck since I got a second chance and you probably know me well enough now to know that I would only muck it up on a monumental scale. I've actually learnt a lot of lessons lately and it's given me a new outlook on life. I started an apprenticeship as a welder, with Tommy Ratson, when I left school. Once I've got my welding certificates maybe I can go off to a far-flung corner of the world and combine my dream of diving and making some money.

Dad's words of wisdom still drive me on, so much so that when he reformed Burnin' Bridges he asked me to be the singer, since the original one had become a dentist!

So if you'll excuse me, we have a charity gig in the market square tonight. It's in support of Mum's environmental group and those albino moles.

THE END